'Sarah—'

'Don't,' she said hus[kily]... should never have [... I] know why it happened.'

'I could hazard a guess. Do you want me to spell it out?'

'No!' She shook herself free of his hands. 'I should have followed my instincts and kept away from you.'

'But you didn't,' Daniel reminded her. 'And you should know that I always carry through whatever I've started, right to the end!'

When **Joanna Neil** discovered Mills & Boon, her lifelong addiction to reading crystallised into an exciting new career—writing romances. Always prey to a self-indulgent imagination, she loves to give free rein to her characters, who are probably the outcome of her varied lifestyle. She has been a clerk, telephonist, typist, nurse and infant teacher. She enjoys dressmaking and cooking at her Leicestershire home. Her family includes a husband, son and daughter, an exuberant yellow Labrador, and two slightly crazed cockatiels.

SMOKE WITHOUT FIRE

BY
JOANNA NEIL

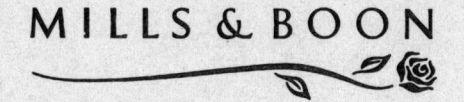

MILLS & BOON

DID YOU PURCHASE THIS BOOK WITHOUT A COVER?
If you did, you should be aware it is **stolen property** as it was reported *unsold and destroyed* by a retailer. Neither the Author nor the publisher has received any payment for this book.

All the characters in this book have no existence outside the imagination of the author, and have no relation whatsoever to anyone bearing the same name or names. They are not even distantly inspired by any individual known or unknown to the author, and all the incidents are pure invention.

All rights reserved including the right of reproduction in whole or in part in any form. This edition is published by arrangement with Harlequin Enterprises II B.V. The text of this publication or any part thereof may not be reproduced or transmitted in any form or by any means, electronic or mechanical, including photocopying, recording, storage in an information retrieval system, or otherwise, without the written permission of the publisher.

This book is sold subject to the condition that it shall not, by way of trade or otherwise, be lent, resold, hired out or otherwise circulated without the prior consent of the publisher in any form of binding or cover other than that in which it is published and without a similar condition including this condition being imposed on the subsequent purchaser.

MILLS & BOON and the Rose Device are trademarks of the publisher. Harlequin Mills & Boon Limited, Eton House, 18–24 Paradise Road, Richmond, Surrey TW9 1SR

© Joanna Neil 1996

ISBN 0 263 79565 9

Set in 10½ on 12 pt Linotron Times 01-9607-50332

Typeset in Great Britain by CentraCet, Cambridge Made and printed in Great Britain

CHAPTER ONE

'Isn't it time you went off to your meeting, Dad? I can manage here if you just turn the sign on the door to "Closed" as you go out.'

Duster in hand, Sarah pulled the stepladder into position in front of the bookcase and began to climb up. It was cramped here in the storeroom but at least she could see through into the shop if need be. Now, though, she scanned the shelves carefully, reading the title on the spine of each book in turn and checking them against a list in her head.

'Are you sure? You've already worked so hard today, keeping an eye on the customers as well as sorting through all the old stock. I don't like leaving everything to you.' William Bryant glanced around the shop with faintly troubled grey eyes before darting a frowning look at his watch.

'I'll be fine and, anyway, there really isn't a lot more I can do here now. Philip will be along soon to pick me up.'

Sarah smiled affectionately down at the top of her father's head, wishing that she could ease some of his anxieties. But he was a reserved man, always keeping things bottled up and holding his worries to himself.

He was in his late fifties and she could see now that his once thick brown hair was beginning to thin at the crown and there were definite streaks of silver around his temples. It was distressing to see how much he'd aged these last few months since he'd battled with the decision to put the shop up for sale.

'You go on,' she said. 'I know how anxious you are to talk things through with the accountant and it's good of him to see you after work like this.'

A flick of the soft yellow cloth brought a shower of dust raining down on her and she coughed and wafted it away with her hand. It was a good thing that she'd thought to bring a change of clothes with her today. As soon as she'd finished this last job she'd take time out to freshen up.

'He's a friend,' her father said absently, still hesitating. 'You know, I thought we might put one or two seventeenth-century maps of the local area on display before morning—that might bring a few more people in—and there was a customer earlier asking about that book of verse—'

'I'm looking for it now, Dad. Don't worry. Go off to your meeting.'

'Well. . .if you think you'll be all right—'

'I do,' she said firmly. 'Off you go.'

He went on his way at last and for the next half-hour she was able to concentrate fully on the task in hand, rubbing her cloth over the old leather-bound volumes and putting to one side the ones that she wanted for tomorrow.

The book of verse was on the top shelf and she reached for it, straining upwards just as the shop's doorbell jangled. Hearing it, she smiled. That had to be Philip. No one else was likely to be dropping by at this time of the evening.

'I'm just finishing off in here, Philip, darling,' she threw back over her shoulder as her fingers closed on the book. 'Why don't you go through to the office and help yourself to coffee while you're waiting? It's freshly made. I just need to get out of these clothes and then I'll join you.'

'Now, that,' drawled a deep, huskily edged male voice, 'has to be the best offer I've had all day.'

It was definitely not the voice that Sarah had been expecting. It tingled over her spine in a way that was distinctly unsettling and Sarah's head turned in shock, her startled gaze running over the tall figure of the man who stood framed in the open doorway of the storeroom. Warm colour rushed into her cheeks.

The man was a stranger to her and his broad shoulders and lean, muscled body were enhanced by the expert cut of his grey suit. He wore the jacket open, revealing a dark shirt beneath. Immaculate trousers encased long legs and she could see that his shoes were of hand-tooled black leather.

Slowly her glance lifted, to be met by a pair of gleaming, amused blue eyes. She turned around to face him properly then, her hand gripping the arched top of the stepladder for support.

'You're not Philip,' she said.

'Regrettably, no.' His glance moved over her, wandering with lazy interest over the curve of hip and thigh outlined by her slim-fitting navy skirt and lingering on the long, honey-gold shapeliness of her legs which was emphasised by the slender elegance of high-heeled shoes. 'Though I could always change my name,' he offered.

Sarah's chin rose as she studied him. The wretched man was determined to take full advantage of her unfortunate slip. Ought she to be on her guard, alone in the shop with someone like this? She wasn't unduly worried, though. That course she'd taken in self-defence had provided her with a few tactics to use in an emergency.

'I hardly think that will be necessary,' she said stiffly.

Carefully she gathered up the pile of books she had selected, holding them to her under one arm as she started down the steps. It was a precarious move at the best of times and it didn't help matters that he was watching her every bit of the way. She glanced down, negotiating the next foothold with the toe of her shoe and turning her ankle a little as her heel encountered the edge of the narrow metal bar.

The man came forward to help her, his hands curving firmly around her arms. The touch of his strong fingers was warm against the thin silk of her blouse and it was oddly disturbing, unexpectedly intimate. She was glad of the wedge of books that separated them.

'Thank you,' she said, when her feet were once more firmly on the ground. 'I can manage now.'

'Are you sure?' He sounded doubtful and didn't seem in any hurry to let her go.

'Quite sure,' she muttered, extricating herself carefully from his steadying grip.

At least he was no longer blocking the doorway and Sarah walked out into the main area of the shop, putting the books down on the polished wooden counter next to the old-fashioned till. It was a relief to be away from the confined space of the storeroom.

'The shop is actually closed,' she pointed out. 'Perhaps you didn't notice the sign on the door?'

'The sign reads "Open",' he returned easily. 'Did you forget to change it?'

'Drat,' she muttered. 'I asked my father to do it but he must have been preoccupied.'

'The door wasn't locked either,' he commented, 'but I expect that was for Philip's benefit?'

A half-smile touched his well-shaped mouth, the strong lines and hard angles of his face changing in a way that stirred a peculiar notion of recognition in her mind. Perhaps he wasn't such a stranger after all. Had she met him somewhere before? Fleetingly she debated the idea but then dismissed the thought. She'd surely have remembered...

Beneath the healthy-looking suntanned glow of his skin his jaw showed a darker hue, the beginnings of a five-o'clock shadow. His hair, she saw, was black, cut short and glittering like jet where the light from the overhead lamp caught it.

'Philip will be here at any moment now,' she told him, frowning, and hoped that he would take the implicit warning on board. The instant that she'd set eyes on him her alarm system had been triggered and she wasn't taking any chances. She had a strong suspicion that this man harboured all the instincts of an animal on the prowl. 'In the meantime, can I help you in some way?'

He didn't look as though he ever needed to rely on other people for anything. There was something about him that made her feel sure that he was a man who was used to taking what he wanted, to being in control, though she wasn't quite certain just what it was that made her so convinced of this. Maybe it was something about his eyes...

Again there was that strange, elusive fragment of recognition before her head cleared once more. Even so, Sarah had the feeling that his indolent, relaxed manner hid the real man and masked an alert, astute mind.

'A cup of coffee would go down well,' he murmured, a flicker of light dancing in his eyes as his gaze skimmed her slender figure, 'but I suppose that's off, too?'

She drew in a sharp breath and decided to ignore his baiting. She had no intention of inviting him to get his feet under the table. Give this man an inch and he'd more than likely take a couple of miles.

'As I said,' she repeated, with just a touch of frost, 'we're closed... But I do have a few things to get on with while I'm waiting for my lift home and if you only wanted to take a quick look around the shop before I lock up you're welcome to go ahead.' She couldn't in all conscience turn a customer away and it was beyond her to think what other purpose he would have in being here.

'May I?' He sounded pleased by the suggestion, as though he hadn't expected it, and that threw her momentarily. 'I'd like that,' he went on. 'From what I saw as I came in, you have some interesting books on display.'

'We deal in special editions and original volumes. If there was anything specific you had in mind. . .?'

'Not particularly.' He seemed in no hurry to move but stayed where he was, casually casting his glance around. Evening sunlight filtered through the bow window, distorted by the thick bull's-eye panes of glass, and dappled the sturdy mahogany bookshelves. 'Sleepy sort of place this, isn't it?' he said.

'I suppose you might say that,' Sarah answered tautly, not quite able to stem the swift tide of defensiveness that welled up in her. She followed the direction of his gaze and wondered if she would ever come to see the shop through a stranger's eyes. There *was* a picturesque, olde-worlde charm about the building and there was no denying that there was an air of slumbrous quiet to the place.

Her father loved it here. Whenever she thought of his decision to sell the shop, she was filled with a sharp sense of regret. He'd worked so hard to make a go of things and now it must soon all come to an end. What was he going to do? He'd be lost without the shop.

With an effort she dragged her attention back to the man. 'We do have our busy times,' she told him.

'But not quite enough of them to make a difference,' he commented drily, looking about him at the 'Reduced' notices that had been pinned up.

Sarah shot him a narrow, dark-eyed glance. 'I

thought you wanted to take a look around,' she said, her voice curt.

Takings had never been high and she'd often wondered whether she ought to find work somewhere else but her father had always squashed that suggestion flat whenever she had broached it.

She knew about the books, he said, and he needed her to do the repairs. She was skilled at it and he trusted her to do a good job. Besides, he was often out—buying, locating certain editions—and he felt secure knowing that she was here.

For all that, he was a worried man. She'd guessed that a few months back, though he obstinately refused to confide in either her or Aunt Margaret.

The letter that had arrived a few days ago hadn't helped either. Thinking back, she remembered how she'd watched the sudden paling of her father's features and had asked him what was wrong but he wouldn't say. He had pushed the letter into his pocket and all she had to go on was a glimpse of a slashing, black signature and an embossed 'Houghton Wood Estate' letterhead which meant nothing to her.

The man beside her moved to pick up one of the silk-bound books from the counter, turning it over in his hands and then leafing through it with careful absorption.

'I like old books,' he said. 'There's such a marvellous sense of history locked up in them; in the way they were produced, in the care that was taken over them—there's no comparison with the mounds of stuff that are churned out today, is there?'

'I can't say that I agree entirely with that,' Sarah murmured. 'Some of the illustrated books being brought out nowadays are very attractively presented and the children's books you see on sale are beautiful, a joy to look at.'

'Hmm... I imagine that's the reason for this closing-down sale,' he said, and when Sarah's finely arched brows drew together he went on, 'Too much competition from the town bookshops. Not many people will be interested in the kind of stuff you have here. Don't you feel that you're in the wrong location, way out here in a village?'

'Wellbrook's almost a small town,' she said defensively.

'It isn't exactly a teeming metropolis, though, is it? Wouldn't you expect to do better closer to the city?'

'People don't go shopping for antique books the way they do for groceries,' she retorted. 'Besides, city rates are exorbitant.'

'Maybe.' His noncommittal murmur did nothing to soothe her slightly rattled feelings. He was looking around again, taking everything in, his shrewd glance moving over the ancient but well-polished counter and the solidly built bookstands. 'The property certainly seems to be a good, sound enough proposition but out here something like a baker's shop might have been more the thing. I expect there was already one established, though.'

Clearly he was thinking aloud and his gaze had begun to roam again, sliding over glass-fronted cabinets and the old grandfather clock which stood in one corner of the room. 'Diversification,' he mused. 'That's probably the answer. Don't put all your eggs into one basket.'

'You seem very knowledgeable on the subject,' Sarah remarked a little stiffly. 'Are you in the property business—or perhaps you're simply interested in this one? If you'd said so earlier I would have directed you to our agent. I can give you his phone number if you like.'

'Heavens, no. I'm not here to buy the place.' He studied her briefly. 'You're a prickly soul, aren't you? Is that because you have something of yourself invested in this place? You're not just a worker here; you're part of the family, aren't you?'

'My father owns the shop.' It was something she dearly wanted to take pride in but the fact that her father was right now talking to the accountant left her feeling suddenly intolerably depressed. Just a few days ago he had painstakingly marked down the prices of all the books in the shop and it had seemed such a gesture of defeat when they were practically giving them away as it was. Some of these volumes were so old and precious, with their own long histories of treasured possession.

After years of trying to build this business up, all his enterprise and resolve had come to nothing. Now this stranger had come in, glanced around, and sized up the situation in less than two seconds and it irked her enormously that he could do that and be so dismissive about it.

'How long have you worked for him?' The man was also doggedly persistent.

'Three years. Since I finished my course at university, though I've always helped out at weekends and in the holidays.'

Sarah couldn't think why she was telling him this, answering all his questions, and when he asked, surprised, 'You've a degree?' her response was sharp.

'Is there anything particularly odd about that?'

He wasn't at all put out by her impatient tone. 'Hardly. But if that's so you must clearly be wasted here.'

'Must I?' she tossed back. 'I'd say that's a debatable point but I really don't think it need concern you. Might I suggest that you use what time there is left to look around? I have work to do.' With that, she determinedly picked up a pile of books and took them over to the display stand where she set about arranging them on the shelves.

If her car hadn't let her down this morning she wouldn't be in this situation now. She could have simply sent this distracting man on his way and set off for home, instead of having to rely on Philip to come for her. As it was, she was left with time on her hands.

Her glance went to the window but there was still no sign of his car outside. She checked her watch. He was very late but there was no point in going to wait for a bus. They were so infrequent that it would be another hour before the next one came along.

It would have been useful if she'd been able to make a start on the bookbinding repairs a customer had asked for but since the supplies she needed to do the job hadn't been delivered as promised that was a complete non-starter. First thing in the morning she'd give the firm another call and they'd better watch out because she'd tell them exactly what she thought of them and she wouldn't be mincing her words. The order had been marked 'Urgent' and there was simply no excuse for such negligent service.

Frowning, she started back towards the counter and found herself in a sudden collision, her soft curves making a mind-shattering fusion with a hard, unyielding male body. The man's hand closed around her waist, his palm flattening in the small of her back.

The shock of that heated contact sent her pulses leaping in wild, frantic disorder and she moved jerkily, her fingers flattening against his chest in her efforts to back away.

But Sarah wasn't going anywhere. He stared down at her, holding her still and watching as the warm colour ran across her cheekbones, and then his free hand lifted to stroke her hair, lightly brushing the chestnut silk at her temple.

'Get your hands off me,' she mouthed fiercely. He was taking liberties and if he didn't stop it in the next fraction of a second she'd aim a sharp kick at his shin.

'Of course,' he said, a mocking twist to his mouth as he slowly brought his fingers down and showed her the filmy strands of cobweb that he had removed from her hair. 'Though I might point out that *you* were the one who bumped into *me*,' he added smoothly as he finally released her. 'You weren't looking where you were going. Too much on your mind, perhaps?'

'A cobweb? Ugh.' She shuddered, her shoulders wriggling as she flicked at the silk of her blouse in distaste. 'I hate cobwebs. I knew I should have changed.'

If only Philip would hurry up and get here. All she wanted to do now was to go back to the cottage and sink into a warm bath. She'd give him another ten minutes, that was all, and then she'd walk the three miles home.

'You look fine to me,' he said, a smile edging around his mouth, 'though if you'd really like to—'

'*Please* don't say it,' she cut in before he could add to her embarrassment. She knew very well what he was thinking and she wasn't going to remove so much as her nail varnish with this man anywhere around. Pulling herself together, she said, 'It's getting late and I really do have to be thinking about locking up now. If you've finished looking around...' She left the sentence open, hoping that he would take the hint and go.

'Uh-huh.' He leaned with easy negligence against the counter, showing no inclination whatsoever to take his leave of her. 'So when this place closes you'll be out of a job. Could be just a few weeks, I guess. Have you given any thought to what you're going to do?'

'Of course I've given it some thought.'

Sarah said it snappishly and immediately regretted her tone because it wasn't at all like her to lose her cool. For some reason, though, her nerves were fraying badly and it didn't help that this man had the unerring quality of being able to put his finger on exactly what was plaguing her.

What *was* she to do when the shop changed hands? What was she actually qualified for when all she had ever done was to work in this quiet bookshop in a place that this aggravating man clearly classed as some kind of backwater settlement?

He was studying her thoughtfully now and she was irritably aware that he must have absorbed her unguarded response and accurately interpreted it.

'It must be difficult for you,' he remarked evenly, 'if this is all you've ever been used to.'

'Please don't concern yourself over my problems,' she said, making an effort to assert herself. 'I can manage quite well to sort them out on my own.' She wanted to lock up and it was high time that this man was on his way. 'If nothing here has caught your attention I really must ask you to leave. My lift should be arriving at any moment and I need to make sure the place is secure before I go.'

'You said that half an hour ago,' he pointed out, with irrefutable and maddening accuracy. 'I think you should sack him. As far as lifts go he seems to be pretty unreliable.'

'If I wanted your opinion I'd ask for it,' Sarah told him frankly. 'Now, if you don't mind, I have to go.'

'It seems to me,' he went on, undaunted, 'that he's the main reason behind your irritability. He's left you stranded here and you've had enough of being at work for one day. That's why you're feeling short-tempered. Now if you'd—'

'I'm sure Philip will be here soon,' Sarah told him firmly. She turned away from the counter and began to search for her bag and keys. 'And, even if he isn't, I'm perfectly capable of getting home under my own steam. I've already told you that I'm ready to lock up but you seem to be remarkably deaf to my hints. Will you please leave?'

The blunt request had no tangible effect on him. 'You know,' he murmured, 'you were wrong in what you said just now. I wouldn't go so far as to say that nothing had captured my attention.' Devilment sparked in his eyes. 'Perhaps I should stay and keep you company until your lift arrives?'

It seemed to Sarah that his lazily sensual appraisal of her was altogether too open and somehow a little shocking. Her blue-grey eyes took on a smoky tint.

'You do know where the door is, don't you?' she enquired in an acid tone. 'Or maybe I should show you the way?'

Unexpectedly he laughed, a husky, throaty rumble that played mischievously over her senses and made her heartbeat quicken its tempo despite her efforts to stay unaffected. She was uncomfortably aware that she was alone here—and vulnerable. Her fingertips pressed tightly into her palms.

'Mr—'

'Daniel,' he said. 'Please call me Daniel.' Taking in her distracted expression, he added, 'I'm sorry, that was unfair of me. It's just that I find it hard to imagine myself being thrown out of the place by a slip of a girl who looks as though she might be blown over in a strong breeze.'

'Looks can be deceptive,' she informed him, recovering some of her poise. 'Now, if you don't mind...'

'You have to get on. Yes, of course. Actually, I did come here for a reason.' He glanced around. 'I had a parcel with me when I came in but I put it down on a table somewhere. Seeing you reaching up to that top shelf took everything else from my mind for an instant. You do have the most fantastic legs.'

His mouth curved at the recollection and Sarah sent him a seething look, which only served to amuse him more. He moved away from her and for the first time she noticed a brown package next to the clock in the corner. 'Here it is,' he said, bringing it back with him and handing it to her. 'Some supplies you ordered, I think.'

Sarah studied the label on the parcel and felt a surge of annoyance growing in her at his casual manner.

'How right you are,' she said tersely. 'It's the supplies I ordered, that's true enough.' Anger sparked in her gaze and there was a cutting edge to her voice. 'And they're late. Five whole days late. You weren't even here before closing time. What did you expect to do if the place had been locked up?'

'I suppose I'd have come back in the morning,' Daniel ventured calmly, but Sarah was in no mood to be appeased.

'Do you realise,' she rebuked, 'that your firm

could have lost me a customer through its sluggish attitude to deadlines? I specifically said that I needed these urgently. The customer wants some very delicate repairs made on a two-hundred-year-old book—for a very special anniversary—and now I'm going to have to work under pressure to make sure I get them done in time.'

'You know about bookbinding?' he queried, his tone interested. 'That's a very specialised occupation.'

'I do.' Her voice was crisp. 'And I pride myself on giving a good service.'

He nodded. 'I'm sure you do.'

'I've *never* been put in the position of having to let a customer down.'

'That wouldn't do at all, would it?' Daniel said, shaking his head in sympathy.

'Certainly not. I've a good mind to send in a letter of complaint.'

'That sounds like an excellent idea.'

Sarah frowned at him. 'Do you think you could stop agreeing with me? It's beginning to sound remarkably patronising.'

'I beg your pardon. It wasn't intended. Perhaps I should explain—'

'The trouble with this country,' she cut in tautly, not caring in the least if she was beginning to sound like Aunt Margaret on her soapbox, 'is that nobody cares any more; nobody pays any attention to detail, to honouring contracts. Well, let me tell you that I do. I believe in keeping my word and abiding by my commitments. Obviously your firm doesn't share the same standard.'

She glared at Daniel and he said consideringly, 'You were much nicer to me when you thought I was Philip. And he's late, you know. At least an hour, by my reckoning.'

She was not going to be put off her stroke. 'So are you. By a lot more.'

'Actually,' he murmured, 'I don't really have any connection with the firm. I just happened to be in the office talking to a friend of mine when I heard your problem being discussed. It struck a chord with me because I needed some repair work done, too: that's why I'd called in on my friend—to see if he knew anyone who could help out. There's been some mix-up with rotas, I believe. A couple of drivers phoned in sick and one of the lorries had broken down. I was travelling up this way so I offered to help out.'

Sarah stared at him. 'You offered—'

'It was no trouble at all,' he said agreeably. 'Though I would have appreciated a cup of coffee. I've been on the road for a good part of the afternoon—there was a lot of holiday weekend traffic on the motorway and an accident was causing a long tailback. Otherwise I'd have been here sooner.'

Sarah swallowed carefully, mortification making her mouth and throat suddenly parchment-dry. She was assailed by guilt at the way she'd treated him.

'It looks,' she began, stiffly hesitant, 'as though I owe you an apology. I'm really very sorry. I jumped to conclusions and I shouldn't have gone on at you like that... It was very good of you to bring the parcel for me...though I think you might have said something sooner.'

She finished on a chagrined note because she'd made an almighty fool of herself and he *was* partly to blame for that. Manners, though, dictated that she make amends and she added bleakly, 'Of course you're welcome to a cup of coffee.'

'That's very kind of you,' Daniel murmured, his tone carefully bland. 'Where is it? Through there?' He indicated the small room at the back of the shop which served as an office-cum-kitchenette.

'Yes. I'll show you.'

Sarah started forward awkwardly, discovering too late that he hadn't moved with her and that he was much closer to her than she had realised. She couldn't help noticing that the top button of his shirt was undone, exposing the bronzed column of his strong throat. She could almost feel the warmth of his skin and the faint essence of a pleasing masculine cologne wafted between them, teasing her nostrils delicately.

It was so different from the brand that Philip used, she noted idly. Philip always used the same kind, one that seemed to her to be heavy and rather sickly sweet.

The phone started to ring in the other room and she gave a small start, her wavering senses rapidly coming back to the present.

'Perhaps you could help yourself to a drink,' she suggested, 'while I answer that?'

His mouth slanted in acknowledgement. 'I'll pour one for you too while I'm about it, shall I? Let me guess,' he murmured thoughtfully, a fiendish humour in the way he studied her, 'you take cream but definitely no sugar.'

What was that supposed to imply? That she had a sharp tongue? She felt like scowling at him and wished that she could have denied him that small victory. Instead, she nodded briefly and said in a curt tone, 'How clever of you to work that out. You'll find I've left everything ready on a tray in there.'

He was already walking towards the office, his stride long and rangy and reminding her uncomfortably, as she followed him, of a large, predatory jungle cat.

Broodingly Sarah watched him, reaching across the desk for the phone as he lifted the coffee-pot. She settled herself, half sitting and half leaning on the polished surface, and picked up the receiver.

'Philip,' she said, hearing his familiar voice. 'Is everything all right? I was beginning to worry.'

Daniel pushed a coffee across the table towards her and she might have managed to smile her thanks, except that it seemed to her he was taking an inordinate interest in the taut stretch of skirt over her thigh and she gave him a quelling stare instead.

Seeing his lips quirk in wry amusement, she felt an unreasoning resentment well up in her. He was incorrigible. How *could* Philip leave her stranded here in the clutches of this...this...tiger?

CHAPTER TWO

'Would you prefer it if I went into the other room while you take your call?' Daniel offered, but Sarah shook her head, impatiently waving him back to his coffee. She might wish that he wasn't here at all but it wasn't going to make any difference to her conversation with Philip. She wasn't going to be exchanging sweet nothings while that man was anywhere in the neighbourhood.

'Darling, I'm sorry about this,' Philip said, his soft voice breaking in on her dark thoughts. 'Things have been really hectic here. Are you OK?'

'Of course I am. What's happened? Another breakdown?'

A couple of feet away from her Daniel leaned back against a cupboard and raised his cup to his lips to take a long swallow of the hot liquid. Sarah watched the movement of his throat with unwilling fascination, her fingers twisting around the phone wire until Philip spoke again and she blinked, shaken out of her abstraction. Frowning, she swivelled around as far as the cable would allow, turning her back on the man.

'We're having trouble with the machines at one of the factories,' Philip was saying. 'I've had to race over to town to deal with it. I do hate having to let you down like this but I'm afraid I'm not going to be able to pick you up after all.'

'I suppose it can't be helped,' Sarah said. It was typical of Philip that he'd dropped everything and gone to deal with this new situation as soon as it had cropped up, though she couldn't help wishing that he had found time to phone her earlier. Perhaps she would call a taxi to get her home—but, then again, a walk might do her good. It had been warm all day and it was going to stay a fine evening from the looks of things. 'Have you managed to sort out what the problem is?'

'No, not yet. In fact, I'm not sure that I can completely. We really need to get in new machinery here. The other factories have been updated to a certain extent and I think the time has come to do the same with this one. I'm going to talk to my father about it this evening. It's long overdue.'

'Won't he be busy working on his speech for tomorrow?' She smiled, visualising Maurice Prescott-Searle preening himself for the day. 'He hasn't talked of anything but the Open Day at Waterleys for the last couple of weeks.'

'He won't be making the speech after all,' Philip said. 'We managed to get hold of Courtenay to do the honours.'

'Courtenay?' she echoed. A little knot of tension worked its way into her brow.

'I did tell you we were trying to get him.' The faint undertone of reproach in his voice wasn't lost on Sarah. 'We wanted someone special, a celebrity who knows all about wildlife. We are trying to raise money for the conservation fund, after all, and he'd be guaranteed to draw a crowd.'

'Yes, I know, but—' Sarah rubbed a hand across her temple as though somehow that might send the tension away '—you said he was out of the country. It was impossible to reach him, you said. There was no chance, that's why your father—'

'His schedule was changed. They finished filming ahead of time, or something along those lines, and he agreed to come along. My father and I rushed around putting up posters yesterday evening and it went out on the local news.' He paused, then added with a trace of impatience, 'You must have heard, Sarah, surely?'

'No,' she muttered, her fingers clenching on the phone wire, her mind busily working. 'I had no idea.'

Philip sighed, and said testily, 'I don't know where you are these days. I've talked to you about this project, tried to involve you in it, but you seem to be miles away sometimes.'

'I've had a lot on my mind lately.' She turned slowly around and looked across the room at the man, her blue-grey eyes narrowing. It couldn't be true, could it? That feeling of recognition she'd had earlier had simply been a figment of her imagination. . .hadn't it?

Daniel slowly put down his cup and returned her stare, one dark brow lifting in silent query.

'Anyway,' Philip said, 'you'll meet Courtenay tomorrow. I'll introduce you and you can do your best to charm him for us. Perhaps that way he'll stay around longer and keep the crowds milling around the stalls. I must go now, Sarah—the engineer wants a word with me.'

He cut the call soon after that and Sarah sat for a moment, unmoving, staring down at the phone.

'Is anything wrong?' Daniel asked. 'Do I take it the boyfriend isn't coming?'

Sarah's head lifted. 'Courtenay,' she said flatly. 'Daniel Courtenay. That's you, isn't it?'

He watched her mouth make a faint grimace and answered, 'For my sins, yes. Why, does that bother you?'

Inwardly she groaned. Charm him, Philip had said. The very thought made her stomach flip over. Fat chance there was of that, anyway, since only a few minutes ago she'd torn him off a strip for being an errant delivery driver.

'I didn't recognise you,' she said crossly. 'You don't look at all the way you do on TV.' Perhaps today was just one of those days when she had been destined from the outset to make a complete idiot of herself.

'It's the hair, I expect,' he agreed, pleasantly enough. 'I decided it was time I did away with the windswept look and invested in a decent haircut.'

'The clothes are different, too,' she pointed out. 'You're usually in desert gear, or windcheater—or whatever fits the climate where you are at the time.' But it wasn't just that, she realised. It had more to do with the clear brilliance of his eyes and the hard, angular good looks that no television picture or grainy newspaper photograph could ever hope to do justice to. Close up, his clean-cut features knocked you for six.

'You've watched my programmes, then?'

'Who hasn't?' she returned.

'I'm flattered you think I have such a wide audience,' he murmured. 'What do you think of them?'

'I hardly think you need my opinion. You must get plenty of people writing in, telling you their views.'

'But I'd still like to know yours,' Daniel persisted.

Her fingers tightened into a little ball. 'I'm sure you don't need me to tell you they're the very best of their kind,' she said tersely.

'I'm glad you think so. Did any particular programme stay in your mind?'

Sarah thought about that for a moment. Clearly he took a great deal of care over his work and, perhaps, as someone for whom perfection was a necessity he was constantly analysing and reviewing what he had achieved.

'There was one,' she answered evenly. 'It was about birds—the hummingbird, especially. I thought the photography was stunning. I remember you said that the hummingbird had to keep searching for nectar for nearly twenty-four hours a day to satisfy its needs...and I thought it would have done a whole lot better to have a rest and conserve its energy: then it wouldn't have needed to eat so much.'

His mouth twisted at that. 'It seems to me that the bird doesn't share your simple logic.'

'Obviously not.'

'So, do you enjoy watching wildlife programmes?'

Sarah gave a light shrug. 'I suppose I do. Though I think they can be quite harrowing at times. Most of them seem to concentrate brutally on the fight for survival—either that or mating, or both.'

'Two basic instincts that apply throughout the animal kingdom, wouldn't you agree? I doubt that people are much different beneath the civilised veneer.'

She didn't miss the devilish glitter in those deep blue eyes and she said coolly, 'Then perhaps it's just as well the veneer stays in place most of the time.'

Daniel laughed. 'Did I hit a sore spot? Poor Sarah, it doesn't seem to be your day, does it? Never mind, just for giving me an honest opinion you earned yourself a lift home. Are you ready to go? My car's outside.'

'There's no need for you to put yourself to any trouble,' she declined politely. 'The walk will keep me fit.' Being alone with Daniel Courtenay for any longer than was absolutely necessary could well turn out to be an exercise fraught with danger. She had only known him for a short time but that had already been quite long enough to confirm her opinion that he had all the sharply honed instincts of the animals he studied.

'Scared?' he challenged, eyes glinting as he read her expression.

'Not at all,' she said in a tight voice. 'You've spent the last hour making a fool out of me and I need the exercise to work off my bad temper. You might have said who you were, right from the start.' It occurred to her suddenly that a moment ago he'd called her Sarah and her lips parted on a swift intake of breath. She hadn't told him her name.

'I had no intention of making a fool of you,' he denied. 'On the contrary, it suits me very well if people don't recognise me. It means that I can come and go once in a while without my plans being disrupted...and you really ought not to be giving me so much hassle, you know. You *are* supposed to be charming me, aren't you?'

Warm colour swept into her face. He had been listening in the whole time. He had absolutely no shame whatsoever.

'That was a private conversation,' she muttered. 'You had no right to be listening in—and I have no intention of charming you. The very thought would be enough to bring me out in a rash.'

'Pity,' he murmured. 'It might have been interesting having you try.'

She slanted him a withering look. 'Forget it,' she said. 'Put that idea right out of your head.'

Daniel laughed again. 'Come on,' he said. 'Stop trying to be so fiercely independent and go and get your coat or whatever. You've been here long enough for one day and I imagine your evening meal's way off schedule. Do you want to stop off somewhere to eat?'

'I'm really not hungry,' she said airily. 'Besides, I have to get home. My father will be expecting me.'

'Yes, I should have thought of that.' A muscle flickered in his jaw, his mouth firming into a faintly grim line. 'He'll be expecting me, too, later on.'

'I beg your pardon?'

'Your father and I have some business to discuss this evening.'

Sarah looked at him in surprise and disbelief. 'My father and you?'

'Your father is William Bryant, isn't he?'

'Well, yes, but he's never mentioned that he knows you or that you had any dealings with each other.'

'I'd managed to work that out for myself,' he said drily, and her eyes narrowed at the hard edge of cynicism in his voice.

'What kind of business do you have with him?'

Daniel shook his head. 'If he hasn't mentioned it already then I think I should leave it up to him to decide how much he wants you to know. Shall we go? Are you ready now?'

There were a lot of questions that she would have liked answered but there was little point in standing around trying to get anything more out of him. He'd said all he was going to say on the subject and she reflected soberly that he and her father had that much in common, at least; they kept their cards close to their chests. As to accepting a lift from him, it seemed that she might as well since it looked as though they both had the same ultimate destination in mind.

His car was a gleaming, low-slung model parked alongside the pavement at the front of the shop. Inside it smelt of leather and opulence and she fastened her seat belt, trying to relax and at least enjoy the comfort. The engine growled into life and as Daniel reached down to change gear she moved her legs hastily to one side. His mocking glance met hers and she looked away quickly, pretending an interest in the scenery as they pulled out into the road.

Sarah couldn't think why it was that he affected her in such an odd way; why her senses jerked in confused reaction to his nearness. It must be that she was tired because of all the anxiety about her father and the shop and she wasn't her usual self.

She never felt that way with Philip—or any other man, for that matter. She knew where she was with Philip. He was a good man, hard-working and practical, and she could relax with him, loving him and knowing that he loved her in return. He would never do anything to make her feel unsettled or on edge. Whereas this man—

She eased herself closer to the window, thankful that Daniel Courtenay didn't appear to expect her to make conversation with him—apart from giving him instructions about the route. It was a relief when the stone-built cottage came into view and she was able to tell him to pull up outside.

Sudden reservations crowded in on her mind. 'Are you sure my father's expecting you?' she asked, her hand on the doorlock. 'It isn't like him not to tell me.'

'Quite sure,' he said, and there was a darkness about his eyes that sent a tiny shiver running down her spine.

'Then I suppose you'd better come in,' she suggested doubtfully.

She slid out of the car and walked to the front

door, breathing in the fragrance of the honeysuckle that clambered over the wall next to the porch. Usually, whatever mood she was in, that sweet scent lifted her spirits but this evening it seemed that nothing was going to do that. She had been feeling decidedly edgy ever since Daniel had said that he needed to talk to her father.

Sarah couldn't imagine what business the two men had to discuss but she couldn't quite rid herself of the suspicion that something wasn't right.

Her father was resting in an armchair in the sitting room, his head tilted back, his eyes closed as though weariness had suddenly overcome him. Amber light from the table lamp played across his face, capturing the leanness of his features and the hollowing of his cheeks. He hadn't been well lately and Sarah hoped that he wasn't suffering a relapse.

She had always thought it strange how very little he and his older sister, Margaret, had in common as far as looks were concerned and, right now, he shared none of her vitality.

From the way that his briefcase was still lying haphazardly on the sideboard, she guessed that he hadn't long been home. He opened his eyes as he heard her walk into the room and she immediately took in his strained expression. Perhaps his meeting with the accountant hadn't gone too well. That was worrying. It had been on her mind for the last few months that the shop must scarcely be breaking even and there were all those bills he'd been pushing to one side...

'Hello, Dad,' she said, injecting a note of cheerfulness into her voice. 'I'm a bit later than usual because Philip couldn't make it in time to pick me up. Do you know Daniel Courtenay? He came by the shop and gave me a lift home.'

Her father looked across the room at her, taking in the tall figure of her companion, and she thought that his skin paled a little as though he'd just received a nasty jolt. It must have been a trick of the light, surely? Why would her father blanch at seeing their visitor? She must be imagining things...or perhaps it was simply the shock of coming face to face with a television personality.

He got to his feet steadily enough, with his hand on the arm of the chair for support.

'Mr Bryant.' Daniel's greeting was quietly formal, his dark eyes coolly assessing the other man.

Her father took in a slow breath and seemed to gather himself up. 'Mr Courtenay. I must thank you for bringing my daughter home.'

'It was my pleasure. And since I was coming this way, anyway...'

'Yes, of course. We must talk, but in private—I think that would be best.'

Sarah frowned, sensing an undercurrent of anxiety in his voice. It was very odd and she wished that she knew what on earth was going on here.

'If you could give me just a few minutes,' her father went on, 'my sister is going away for the weekend on a garden tour with her club and I must see her off. She's running late. She was supposed to have been on her way an hour ago.'

As though she had heard her name being mentioned, Margaret swept into the room like a small hurricane. She was a neat woman, her black hair shot through with grey but cut in a short, layered style that feathered down over her temples and softened the sharp lines of her face.

'I'm just off,' she said, then stopped as she saw the trio gathered in the room. Her glance went to their visitor. 'Good heavens, you're Daniel Courtenay, aren't you? The naturalist? I saw your picture posted up around the village. What are you doing here?'

'He brought Sarah home,' William put in quickly. 'Hadn't you better be going? Do you want me to carry your over-night bag out to the car?'

'There's no need for that. I can manage perfectly well.' She gave her brother a sharp look. 'You seem to be in a great hurry to get rid of me, William. You've been fussing ever since you walked in the front door. Is something wrong?'

He looked away, reaching for his briefcase and sliding loose papers into it from the sideboard. 'Of course not. I thought you had a coach to meet, that's all.'

Sarah watched him deal with the clasp on the case and felt a twinge of dismay. He was definitely not himself. She had sensed it and so had Margaret.

Her aunt turned to Daniel. 'I've always thought your work sounded fascinating. For a young man—what are you, mid-thirties?—you seem to have crammed an awful lot in. What a pity it's the Whit holiday—the children at school would have loved to have you come in and talk to them.'

'My aunt's headmistress at the local primary

school,' Sarah explained. People who didn't know her aunt could sometimes be taken aback by her brisk manner.

'Ah.'

'Perhaps I could phone you about it after the holiday?' Margaret asked.

Daniel Courtenay inclined his head in a polite, almost imperceptible, movement. He wasn't committing himself to anything. 'As you please.'

It was enough to satisfy Margaret. 'You live down South, don't you, on a large, country estate? I remember reading about the farmland and the orchards. I'll give you a call there when I get back.' She glanced around briefly. 'Now, I must be on my way. I hope everything goes well tomorrow at Waterleys. Of course, with the Prescott-Searles organising it, nothing would dare to go wrong.'

She left quickly after that but Sarah's mind was elsewhere as her father left the room to wave Margaret off at the door. She was thinking about a large, country estate and remembering an embossed Houghton Wood letterhead and the discomfiting effect that letter had had on her father.

'Your family home,' she said sharply to Daniel, 'it's on the Houghton Wood Estate, isn't it? You didn't mention that earlier but I should have made the connection before this. I can't think why I didn't.'

'Should you?' He raised a dark brow. 'I don't see that it's of any importance. In any case, my home address is no secret to anyone who reads magazine features. The place has been documented, photographed and laid out for all to see.'

'It isn't your home I'm concerned about,' she remarked tersely. Her father was definitely on edge and the fact that Daniel Courtenay's presence here evidently had something to do with his agitation brought her protective instincts fiercely into play. 'It's the fact that you wrote to my father some days ago and I have the feeling that something is going on here that I should know about.'

His gaze narrowed on her as he said evenly, 'If your father chose not to say anything, then he must have had his reasons. You'll have to ask him anything you want to know.'

Sarah's mouth tightened. 'I'll do that. Take a seat, won't you, Mr Courtenay? I have things to do but I'm sure my father will be with you in a few minutes.'

She walked out of the room, breathing a little faster than usual because she was trying to contain her frustration, and bumped into her father outside his study.

'She's gone,' he announced. He seemed relieved now that Margaret was out of the house and that was strange, Sarah thought, because the two of them usually got along very well together.

'I want to know what's going on,' she insisted. 'What is he doing here, and why didn't you tell me that you were expecting him?'

'I did mean to tell you,' he said, 'but it slipped my mind.'

Sarah pressed her lips firmly together. She didn't believe for one minute that it had slipped his mind. He wasn't a forgetful kind of person, no matter what troubles he was burdened with.

'I know something's wrong,' she said through gritted teeth. 'I can feel it. From the moment I set eyes on him I knew he was trouble and if he does anything at all to add to your worries I'll make him rue the day.'

'No, Sarah.' He looked alarmed at that. 'Whatever happens, you mustn't antagonise him. That's the last thing either of us must do.'

'But *why*? Don't you think I deserve some kind of explanation?'

He seemed to slump wearily. 'It's true enough; I should have told you before this—only I was hoping I could find a way out without anyone getting to hear. I didn't want Margaret to know—I still don't want her to know.'

He swallowed carefully and put a hand to his chest, breathing deeply as though to ease a pain there. 'The thing is, years ago I spent some time on the Houghton Wood Estate and I came to know the family. Daniel's mother lent me money to buy the cottage and finance the shop—'

'Daniel's mother?'

Sarah frowned but William only nodded and moistened his lips a little, before going on, 'To begin with everything was fine; I was able to meet the payments. Only later, with the recession and one thing and another, I needed to borrow more just to keep afloat. Then I started to fall behind with the payments and, as time went on, instead of diminishing the debt started to grow.'

Sarah gasped. 'After all these years—'

'I've never had any problems dealing with

Elizabeth Courtenay—she's always been very understanding—but now it seems that she needs to recover money quickly for a business deal of her own. And I think she's put everything in her son's hands. Daniel Courtenay's here to collect.'

'Oh, Dad...' She paled and put her fingers to her trembling lips. 'What does it mean? What's going to happen—?' Then she put her hand on his, looking at him with stricken eyes. 'Are you saying that we could lose the house—lose everything?' A chill was creeping through her veins.

'I don't know. That's the plain truth of it. If the sale of the shop goes ahead—if I can get him to agree terms—there may be a chance. I have to do something.'

She said shakily, 'Why didn't you say something before this? You know I'd have tried to help. I have some savings. It isn't a lot but, whatever you need, it's yours.'

'No, girl. I would never take your money. Somehow I'll find a way to deal with the situation but, until I can find a way to sort out this mess I've made of things, we have to be very careful around him. Do you understand?'

'Yes,' she said. 'I understand perfectly.'

CHAPTER THREE

DANIEL was standing by the window, browsing through a motoring magazine, when Sarah and her father went back into the sitting room. He put it to one side as they walked in and surveyed them both with cool eyes the colour of slate.

'It occurred to me,' William Bryant said, 'that since time's getting on and we haven't eaten yet, let alone had a chance to talk, perhaps you might care to stay here overnight? Margaret's room is available so it would be no problem.'

Sarah's stomach twisted at her father's words. She was still trying to come to terms with what he had told her and now he was inviting the man to stay under their roof.

'There's really no call for you to make arrangements on my account,' Daniel said with a shrug. 'I'm quite content to stay at the Royal in town.'

'No. I insist. I'm sure that if the Prescott-Searles knew that you had come over to Wellbrook today they would have wanted to put you up themselves. Besides, Waterleys is much easier to reach from here. It would save you a tedious journey in the morning and Sarah would be able to go with you and show you around the place. And if we don't have to watch the clock we'll be much better able to get on with our discussion.'

'Put that way,' Daniel said, 'it would be churlish of me to disagree.' His glance went fleetingly to Sarah, a spark in its blue depths.

She looked away, a sudden warmth flushing her skin. She could well understand her father's tactics. He was a hospitable man by nature but his invitation had an underlying purpose. He most likely thought that if Daniel was a guest in their house he'd be less inclined to be unpleasant about any delay in getting the money that was owed to him.

She wasn't convinced that it would make any difference to the outcome. She was even less sure that Daniel hadn't gauged her father's intent. He was nobody's fool and he'd seen for himself that the shop wasn't seeing much trade.

'Good, that's settled,' William said. 'Will you excuse me for a minute or two while I sort through one or two papers? I'm sure Sarah will fix you a drink.'

Left alone with Daniel, Sarah said, 'What will you have? Scotch?' She went over to the drinks cabinet. 'I expect you're hungry, too. I'll make us something to eat in a moment. I feel I owe you something—it's the least I can do to recompense you for your time and trouble in bringing over my box of supplies.'

'You seem very anxious not to be in my debt in any way,' he commented softly. 'Now, why is that, I wonder?'

His gaze held hers and she felt a ripple of heat surge through her veins, leaving her oddly breathless. 'Anxious?' she repeated huskily. 'That's rather a strong way of putting it. Is being in your debt likely to be such a great problem to me?'

He gave her a crooked smile. 'Who can tell?' he murmured, his glance drifting slowly to take in the oval perfection of her face and coming to linger on the soft, pink fullness of her mouth.

A pulse began to beat heavily in her throat and she had to breathe deeply against the sudden constriction that had arisen in her chest.

'I must see to things in the kitchen,' she muttered. 'You won't mind if I leave you to amuse yourself for a while, will you? There are newspapers in the rack.'

'So I noticed.' Daniel took off his jacket and when Sarah handed him his drink, she said, 'Let me take that. I'll put it on a hanger for you.'

His jacket was warm and smelt faintly of cologne and something quintessentially male. Sarah put it away from her quickly in the small cloakroom under the stairs, then went into the kitchen to see to the meal.

She had already seen to most of the preparations earlier in the day and when everything was served up and ready she called the two men to come and eat. Her father had joined Daniel but she didn't think that they'd been talking business. Daniel was commenting on a news report as he walked into the kitchen where the table was set.

'Aren't you eating with us?' Daniel enquired, his glance taking in the two places that she'd laid.

'I'll have something later. I'm really not that hungry.' It was true enough. Her stomach rebelled at the mere thought of food because she was so anxious about the things that her father had said. 'Excuse me,' she said. 'I must go and freshen up.'

He frowned but stood to one side to let her pass by him and she went out into the hall and up the stairs to her room. She picked out a skirt and matching top from her wardrobe, then hurried into the bathroom to shower. If she could have washed him out of her system she might have felt a lot better but she had to settle instead for a change of clothes and a vigorous brushing of her hair.

Taking fresh linen from the cupboard in the bathroom some twenty minutes later, Sarah went into Margaret's room, stripped the bed of its covers and pushed them into the laundry bin. It might have helped if she could have blamed Daniel for the churned-up way she was feeling but deep down she knew that the biggest problem was her father's financial situation and the worry about how he was to deal with it. Would Daniel accept any arrangement that her father could devise?

'Do you need any help?' The deep, gravel-tinged voice startled her and she swung round quickly to see the object of her thoughts coming into the room. 'You've had a long day and I feel I'm putting you to a lot of trouble.'

She hadn't heard Daniel come up the stairs and the fact that he was here now standing opposite her, those all-seeing eyes taking in her every fleeting expression, put her sharply at a disadvantage. He was carrying a brown leather flight bag, and she guessed that he must have gone out to his car to retrieve it from the boot.

'It's no trouble,' she said, her tone dismissive as she flicked a sheet over the divan. 'I thought you were talking to my father?'

He set the bag down on the floor. 'We'll talk in a while. I can wait. I'm in no hurry.'

No. He was the tiger in the night. Waiting. Knowing that when he was ready, all he had to do was to reach out and take a playful swipe...

He was watching her now. 'Is there anything I can do for you?'

He said it lightly enough but when his glance swept over her in that glittering way of his she found herself struggling with a wild moment of electric tension, her senses leaping in hectic disarray. His presence confused and disorientated her and she wished that he didn't have the ability to affect her this way.

Just knowing that she was alone with him in a bedroom was having a disastrous effect on her nervous system but it wouldn't do to let him see that. At all costs she must keep her cool.

'Nothing, thank you,' Sarah told him, hoping that he would take her at her word and leave. 'I can manage.' Swiftly she folded the corners of the sheet, tucking them neatly under the mattress, conscious the whole time that he was watching her precise movements with curiosity.

'For some reason which is beyond my understanding,' she muttered by way of explanation, 'Aunt Margaret doesn't believe in fitted sheets so I've developed my own way of doing things. I like to make sure everything will stay in place.'

'I can see that,' Daniel said, amusement threading his words. 'You're very efficient. For myself, I just shake things up a little and climb in as it comes.'

She could visualise it well enough and her mouth moved in a wry grimace as she tried to push away the picture his comment invoked. She didn't want to know about his night-time habits. The very thought of them made her go hot all over.

'She doesn't like duvets either,' she informed him briskly, 'but I can find one for you if you like.'

'Don't bother. I agree with Margaret. I much prefer to slide into bed and feel the cool sheets next to my skin, especially at this time of year.'

She wished that he hadn't said that. Her mind seemed to reel as the intoxicating image of his naked, muscular body swam unbidden into her head—tanned and supple, lean and strong. She shook it away, turning to reach for the appliquéd counterpane and desperately hoping that the heated vision had left no tell-tale imprint on her cheeks.

What on earth was the matter with her, to be experiencing such odd reactions ever since he had appeared on the scene? It wasn't like her—it wasn't the way she was at all—to be affected by such fundamentally physical things. Perhaps the looming change in her lifestyle was having a disastrous effect on her hormones. She couldn't think of any other explanation for it and certainly she'd never experienced such graphic and disturbing emotions with Philip.

Sarah loved Philip. It was a quiet, gentle feeling, being in love with him, and she had always been content with the placid, easygoing relationship they shared. What did it matter if there was no sharp, overwhelming peak of ecstasy? It wasn't important, was it?

Anyway, that kind of emotion could quickly burn itself out and surely there was something to be said for a more gentle, uneventful kind of loving? She wouldn't let these doubts crowd in on her. Before this man came along they had scarcely even entered her head.

Thankfully she finished making the bed and turned to leave the room. 'Feel free to put things out on the dressing table,' she said. 'I've cleared some space for you. I've put out fresh towels, too, but if there's anything else you need just ask. The bathroom is next door, on the left.'

'Thanks.'

Downstairs, the doorbell rang and she hurried to answer it, glad of the chance to make her escape.

Philip was waiting there on the doorstep, his handsome face breaking into a smile as she pulled open the door. He was a few inches taller than Sarah, whose own five feet four brought her eyes on a level with his chin.

'I'm on my way home,' he said. 'I just thought I'd drop by for a minute or two.'

She smiled back at him, reassured by his calm, solid presence in her life, happy that he'd taken the time to stop by and see her when she knew that he must have had a trying day.

'I didn't expect to see you until tomorrow afternoon. I thought you'd be much too busy to come here.'

'It's been one hell of a day,' he agreed, 'but I wanted to leave these plants with you for the stall tomorrow. One of the girls at the factory brought them in.'

Disappointment rose in her at the knowledge that he hadn't made a special journey to see her but she forced it back down. Thinking that way was childish. After all, she knew that he was a practical man and that was one of the things she had always liked about him.

'They're lovely,' she said, running her glance over the greenery. 'I'm sure they'll sell like hot cakes.'

'That's the general idea.' He walked into the hall and put the tray of plants down on the low table next to the telephone seat then straightened, brushing his hands to rid them of any plant debris.

Philip was a fastidious man—his brown hair brushed back from his forehead in conservative fashion, his brow high and smooth, his face unlined by any shadow of tension. He knew what he wanted out of life and his course was set straight. Sarah respected him for that. He had a goal and he was working steadily towards it. She was part of the future he had mapped out and that made her feel good about things.

In a couple of months they planned an engagement and, in another year, she would be his wife. If his aims and ambitions didn't quite match her own, what did that matter? They had all the time in the world to sort things out between them.

'It might be easier if you take these plants along with the rest you've been putting by,' he said, 'because I can't guarantee I'll be free to help you set up. Your car will be fixed by then, won't it?'

'I doubt it but I'll sort something out.'

'If you have any trouble ring for a taxi.'

'I will. Did you clear up your problem at the factory?' she asked, looking up at him, wanting to drink in the warmth of his hazel eyes. She wanted him to put his arms around her so that she would feel...safe, secure. Somehow she didn't feel either of those things right now. She felt a little shaken up, out of sorts, and she would have liked his solid frame to cling to.

'I managed to get things fixed temporarily,' he said. 'I'm sorry I wasn't able to bring you home. What did you do...catch a bus?'

'I managed to get a lift. Your celebrity called in at the shop...'

'Courtenay? He's in town?'

'He's here, in Wellbrook. He's staying with us.'

Philip frowned. 'With you? But—'

'My father thought it best,' Sarah supplied, 'and it'll be easier if I go with him to Waterleys from here.'

She turned as she heard a muffled sound behind her and jumped a little as Daniel appeared at her side. She'd had no idea he was there. He'd crept up on her like an animal on the prowl and just knowing how close he was made the skin on the back of her neck prickle in alarm.

She took in a slow breath, trying to calm the swift

leap of her pulse, and carefully made the introductions.

'This is very unexpected, meeting you here,' Philip said, responding to Daniel's quizzical stare. 'I had no idea you were planning on coming over a day earlier or I'd have made suitable arrangements.

'Of course, my father and I were delighted when you agreed to come along to our event. We weren't at all sure that you would be able to spare us the time and, with your own family circumstances such as they are at present, it would have been understandable if you had wanted to turn us down.'

'"Such as they are"?' Sarah repeated, puzzlement in her tone. 'What circumstances? Is this something I ought to know about?'

'I imagine Philip is referring to my father's death a few months ago,' Daniel said, his eyes dark and unreadable.

'I'm sorry,' she said. 'I hadn't heard about that. Had he been ill, or — ?'

'No, he wasn't ill. It was a sailing accident. He was a very fit and agile man and he loved to be out on the water whenever it was possible. A freak storm blew up on this particular day, though, and he was injured trying to bring the boat under control. He went overboard but by the time rescuers got to him it was too late. There was nothing anyone could do.'

'I'm really sorry,' Sarah said again, her eyes troubled. 'Were you with him at the time?'

He shook his head. 'My mother was. They were spending a holiday with friends.'

'It must have been terrible for her.'

'It was. I went out to her on the first flight available and she was absolutely distraught. We were all shocked to the core. They had been married for a good many years and it was a very happy marriage. She was inconsolable.' His own eyes were dark with memories, his expression sober, and Sarah guessed that there had been a deep bond between Daniel and his parents.

'I suppose,' Sarah said quietly, feeling a sharp tug of sympathy for the other woman, 'that there was no time to say goodbye. When something happens suddenly like that the grief must be intense. Is she coping any better now?'

'I think so though she did suffer a severe collapse, both mentally and physically. It didn't help that there were so many legal matters to see to concerning my father's estate and her own business affairs were sliding rapidly out of hand. Of course, she was in no condition to deal with any of them. Her doctor insisted that if she was to recover her health she should get away from everything and take a complete break.'

'Has she done that?'

'She has. She's spending the summer in France with my father's brother and his family.'

'And the estate problems and so on?' Philip queried thoughtfully. 'What will happen about those?' As a businessman himself he could appreciate the difficulties that might crop up.

'I'm dealing with all that, fitting it in where I can in my work schedule. My mother asked me to sort things out for her...' He paused. 'All her business affairs, and that's exactly what I intend to do. My mother will not be disturbed in any way.'

Daniel's gaze shifted to Sarah, and the slate was back in his eyes, making her shiver as if ice water was running through her veins.

She steeled herself not to flinch under that cold scrutiny. 'She must have absolute faith in your abilities,' she murmured.

His mouth made a sardonic twist. 'She's never had reason to doubt them.'

'But it is expected that she'll recover?' Philip asked.

'Hopefully being with my uncle and aunt and their offspring will help her to get her strength back so that eventually she'll be able to take over the reins once more.'

Sarah wondered if that might be the answer to their own problems. Elizabeth Courtenay had always been reasonable, her father had said. Could they hold out long enough until she recovered? Perhaps by then the shop would be sold. Would it bring in sufficient money to pay what was owed? But Elizabeth needed the money now...

'Do your relatives live permanently in France?' Philip was saying. 'Courtenay's a French name, isn't it?'

'That's right, and, yes, they do. My ancestors came over to settle in England a few centuries ago but there are still branches of the family there.'

The two men talked for a while longer about the French countryside and holidays spent on hillside farms but when Daniel heard movement coming from the kitchen he said, 'I must go. I have some business to sort out. No doubt I'll see you tomorrow at Waterleys? I'm looking forward to it. Sarah will be there with me, of course. I'm told she'll act as my guide.' His glance drifted over her, a crooked smile shaping his mouth.

'I'm sure it will be a great success with you there as our guest celebrity,' Philip said.

Daniel inclined his head briefly towards them both then turned, leaving them to watch him as he made his way purposefully along the passage.

'I hadn't realised that he had any family worries,' Sarah mused. 'He seems relaxed enough, considering that he's been under pressure filming these last few weeks on top of everything else.'

'Maybe. Let's just hope he isn't feeling too relaxed.'

She looked at him in surprise. 'That's an odd thing to say. Whatever do you mean?'

His mouth twisted into something that resembled a scowl, which was not at all like the Philip she was used to. 'I don't like the idea of him staying here,' he muttered. 'I'd much rather he was staying at Stoneleigh House with my parents and me. I think you should be careful around him, Sarah.'

'I thought you admired the man,' she said with a frown. 'You couldn't wait to get him to agree to help out with the Open Day, yet here you are warning me against him. I don't think I understand.'

'I respect his work, well enough. There's no disputing he's earned acclaim for that but I'm not blind to the way he conducts his private life. You only have to read the papers to know that he changes his women the way he changes his sheets.'

'Journalistic exaggeration, surely?' Sarah said dismissively. She might not trust Daniel Courtenay any further than the glint in his eye but he couldn't take all the blame for his supposedly libertine existence. When all was said and done, there had to be willing women. 'You don't really believe everything you read in the papers, do you?'

'I believe the saying, "There's no smoke—"' Philip muttered, breaking off as sounds came from along the passageway. 'I'd better go. Just take care, won't you? I'll see you tomorrow, darling.' Bending towards her, he kissed her lightly on the mouth then quickly straightened as her father and Daniel walked towards them. 'I have to be off now, William,' he said. 'Sorry not to have time to stay and talk but I only stopped by for a moment.'

'That's all right, Philip,' William answered. 'I understand. I hope everything goes the way you want it to tomorrow.' To Sarah he added, 'We'll be going into the study for a while. Don't wait up; we may be some time.'

'I won't,' she said. 'I have some work to do in my room.'

Closing the door after Philip, she turned to gaze after her father as he went into the study. He didn't look at all well and there was a faint blueness about his mouth that worried her.

She stopped Daniel as he was about to follow him. 'My father isn't strong,' she told him in a low, warning voice. 'He's recovering from a nasty bout of flu and I don't want him kept up late, no matter what you have to say to each other.'

His eyes narrowed. Coolly he said, 'I'll keep it in mind.'

So she had annoyed him. He didn't like being told what to do, having restrictions imposed upon him, but it couldn't be helped. She couldn't let his black mood bother her. Her father was a good man, even if he had got himself into difficulties, and she'd protect him to the hilt in spite of himself. If Daniel Courtenay didn't like it that was too bad.

Upstairs in her room, she worked on the book repairs for more than an hour before she decided that she had done enough for one day. Stretching to ease the tired muscles in her shoulders and neck, she decided that she might as well put everything tidily away and use the bathroom before the two men came up.

It had been a long, peculiar sort of day and she wouldn't be sorry to get to bed. Maybe her father could sort something out and, tomorrow, when the business of Waterleys was finished Daniel would remove himself from their lives and things could get back to normal. She wouldn't be sorry. Somehow, with him around, everything seemed strangely out of synch. It was very unsettling.

The shower was warm and soothing and she enjoyed the feel of the water slicking over her soft skin. When she had finished she put on a thin cotton nightshirt and slid a robe over her shoulders, loosely tying the narrow belt at her waist before going back into her room.

Once there she sat at the dressing table to dry her hair and then pull a brush through its silken length. Next door she heard someone moving about and guessed that Daniel had come upstairs and was getting ready for bed. Her ears had been tuned for her father's footsteps but so far there had been no sound of him.

A noise of breaking glass shattered the quiet. It had come from downstairs—the kitchen probably—and Sarah quickly abandoned her brush and hurried to see what had happened.

When she reached the kitchen door she found her father kneeling on the tiled floor, brush and dustpan in hand. He looked up at her as she went towards him and she was alarmed to see the grey pallor of his cheeks.

'Dad, what's wrong? Are you ill?'

He straightened up, dropping the contents of the dustpan into a bin in the cupboard. 'No, love. It's nothing. I dropped a glass, that's all. Silly of me. I was just trying to get a drink of water and the thing fell out of my hand. Everything's fine. I'll see to it. You go back to bed.'

His voice seemed strong enough but she was worried, all the same. There had been more than one occasion recently when she had caught a look of pain in his grey eyes and she wasn't convinced when he said that there was nothing wrong.

There was a small tablet bottle on the table and she picked it up, examining the label. 'These are heart pills, aren't they? How long have you been taking them?'

'They're only for the odd twinge,' he said. 'No need for any fuss.'

Sarah stared at him, her expression troubled. 'You shouldn't be under all this strain. It can't be doing you any good. Did you manage to come to any agreement with him? Will his mother wait until the shop's sold?'

He said nothing for a second or two, then slowly bent to clear up the remains of broken glass. 'He put something to me, a kind of ultimatum.'

'What was it? What did he say?'

William finished cleaning up the floor, putting everything tidily away, before he spoke again. 'He's going to pay his mother everything I owe out of his own account. It means that now my debt is solely to him. He's renegotiated the terms and we've agreed payments but, if I can't make any of them, he could call in the whole of the loan at any time.'

Sarah's mouth was dry, her throat aching. 'But how can you pay? Is there enough money coming in?'

'I'll find it somehow. There are one or two insurance policies that I can cash in. I'll find a way to keep going until the shop is sold.'

She sensed the doubt in his voice. 'You know I want to help in any way I can,' she said urgently. 'If you change your mind about my money, if you—'

'I know, and we'll talk again if need be. But not now. I'm very tired, and you must be, too. You go on up to bed now. You've a busy day ahead.'

The subject was closed. He had that look about him that told her there was no more to be gained from talking to him and when he turned away from her to pour himself another drink and toss down a small tablet she reluctantly said goodnight and made her way back upstairs.

Engrossed in her thoughts, she didn't at first see Daniel on the landing.

'Is it your father? Is something wrong?' His glance flicked over her.

She looked up. His shirt was undone as though he had been about to take it off when he had heard the noise and had come to investigate. His chest was bared, his firmly muscled skin tanned and supple—just as she'd imagined—gleaming faintly in the light. Sarah shifted her gaze.

'I worry about him,' she said. 'He's always worked hard, struggled to keep the business going, and he's been keeping things too much to himself, locked away inside.' She tilted her head to look at him squarely. 'He isn't well. If you upset him in any way, I'll. . .'

'You'll what, Sarah?' His glittering gaze locked with hers. 'Believe me, he won't thank you for your interference.'

She sucked in a sharp breath. 'Don't tell me what I can and can't do. I don't care what your dealings are with my father but just bear in mind that if his health suffers in any way because of them I shall do whatever I can to make sure you never get to harass him again.' She swung away from him, intent on heading for her room, but his hand closed on her wrist, stopping her.

'I'll tell you whatever I think necessary. And right

now I think you should calm yourself and accept the simple facts as they are.' Daniel watched the rising heat of her anger and his jaw hardened, a muscle flexing there. 'I want to know what the problem was with your father just now. Is he OK?'

She resisted him as he clamped her other wrist, trying to draw back from the flare of determination that she read in his eyes. Her movements loosened the tie at her waist and the edges of her robe began to slowly drift apart but she scarcely had time to register that fact.

He pulled her towards him and fever pulsed through her veins as she found herself moulded to the lean strength of his long, hard body. She felt the pressure of his taut thighs against her limbs and it left her feeling strangely weak and vulnerable.

'Is he OK?' he repeated, and she gave an awkward shrug, inadvertently dislodging the thin silk of her robe so that it slid down from one shoulder.

'Yes...yes, I think so.' To be scrupulously fair, Sarah couldn't be absolutely certain that Daniel had had anything to do with her father's shockingly pale appearance. She might strongly suspect that he'd had a hand in it but proving it was another matter. Her father had looked ill before this. 'He dropped something, that's all.'

She thought that now that he had made his point he would let her go but she was wrong. The hands that held her did lessen their grip, though, as he smiled down at her, a mocking light in his blue eyes.

'That's a relief then, isn't it? I can breathe easily again now that I know my hide is saved...at least until next time.' Daniel's hands moved lazily over her, gliding over the smooth curve of her spine and settling with warm possession on the rounded swell of her hips. His touch had an almost hypnotic effect on her. It made her feel as though she was floating in space, dizzy and unreal.

She stared up at him, strangely fascinated by the dancing gleam in his eyes and unable to pull away from it, though she sensed there was lurking danger in that unwilling attraction. 'You're making fun of me,' she said huskily.

'You make it so hard for me to resist.' He shifted position so slightly that it was almost imperceptible, except that now her breasts were softly crushed against the hard wall of his chest and she thought that she might never breathe normally ever again. His hand stroked upwards, sliding over her arm in a slow, sensuous path, creating melting pools of heat inside her with every lingering caress.

His long fingers reached out to tangle themselves in the coppery strands of her hair, enclosing its soft weight in his palm. 'You're not so different from your father,' he muttered. 'You appear so very cool on the outside but I think that's just a sham. You've only banked the fire that's smouldering away inside, waiting to be released.'

Sarah felt the brush of his fingers against the nape of her neck and a quivering awareness rippled through her body; an awareness that she wanted desperately to deny.

Her hands pushed at his chest and that was a mistake, she knew straight away, because the feel of his warm skin beneath her fingertips sent an electric jolt through her limbs. She felt light-headed and insubstantial and that wasn't at all the way she wanted to feel around this man.

She drew in a shuddering breath and said, 'I think you have a vivid imagination, Mr Courtenay. Or perhaps you've simply had too much of my father's Scotch. Please let me go.'

Slowly Daniel did as she asked. 'You want to run away and hide, is that it?' His voice was soft and low, enveloping her almost as closely as his arms had done a moment ago.

'From you?' she said, struggling to keep a steady note in her voice. 'That thought hadn't crossed my mind.'

'Hadn't it? I wonder. I wonder what thoughts were occupying Philip's mind when he left this house earlier? I'm sure I wouldn't be so keen to leave the woman I loved after such a short space of time and with such a chaste, cold little kiss as the one he gave you. I think I'd have wanted something much more passionate and expressive to warm me on my way.'

Sarah's eyes flickered smokily. She might well share that view but she wasn't about to let him know that.

'Perhaps it's fortunate, then,' she said with a cool twist to her mouth, 'that we don't all suffer from the handicap of a frenzied libido such as yours. I hardly think it would be appropriate for him to be any more expressive with an audience looking on. Besides which, Mr Courtenay, my relationship with Philip is none of your damn business.'

Her sharp words did not have the desired effect on him. Instead his glance drifted over her face, wandering in leisurely fashion from her widely spaced blue eyes to the rose-tinted fullness of her mouth. 'Isn't it?' he murmured silkily. 'I think you're wrong, Sarah. I think, one way or another, your relationship with Philip is going to be very much my business.'

CHAPTER FOUR

DRAWING back the curtains in her room, Sarah blinked as she looked out onto a bright spring morning, the sky clear and blue with the promise of a long, hot day to come. If only her mind could be as clear and bright, instead of persistently wandering in disconcerting circles.

Waking with the knowledge that Daniel Courtenay was in the house, in the next room, had thoroughly unsettled her but that was hardly surprising. He wasn't a man that you could simply ignore.

The very first moment she had set eyes on him in the shop her senses had leapt in alarm and now every time she thought about him a pulse of heat ran through her veins and sent her mind spiralling off on a dizzying path that could only lead to trouble. It was too nerve-racking to be endured and she couldn't think why it was happening to her.

She had simply been overreacting to everything that had happened the day before; that was all. Anyway, she couldn't think what he'd meant by that last parting shot. He was no threat to her or Philip; how could he be?

It was strange how little comfort or satisfaction she found in telling herself that. How could she keep from worrying about her father? He'd said that he would find the money he owed but she couldn't think how he was going to do that.

In any case there was little she could do about it at the moment, except be thankful that after today Daniel would be on his way back to Houghton Wood. From then on it wasn't likely that she would see much of him. Was it?

In the meantime, there was only one thing to do. She would start this morning afresh and treat him with exactly the same courtesy that she would have shown to any of the customers who walked into the shop.

Some twenty minutes later he came into the kitchen as she was sliding toast onto the rack. He had exchanged his suit for dark trousers and a cool-looking sports shirt; clothes which, despite being casual, still managed to give off that same air of quality and expensiveness. From the damp gleam of his hair it was clear that he must have showered and his clean-shaven, angular good looks were somehow brought even more sharply into focus. He was a dangerously attractive man.

It made her feel twitchy just to be near him and that bothered her more than a little because it wasn't something that she'd ever experienced before. She had always been relaxed around Philip and that was the way it should be, wasn't it? She was content with him. He was all she had ever looked for in a man and there was no reason on earth why she should go hot all over just being in the same room with Daniel Courtenay.

'I must have overslept,' he greeted her. 'All this

good, country air must be affecting me. I haven't felt so refreshed and invigorated for a long time.'

Sarah sent a glance his way from under thick, dark lashes. It was true enough; you could almost feel the energy and vitality that radiated from him and that did absolutely nothing to make her feel any easier about having him around.

'I hope you like scrambled egg,' she said, 'because that's what I had planned for breakfast. Help yourself to coffee and fruit juice.'

'Hmm. It smells good.' He glanced around the kitchen, taking in every detail of the clean, scrubbed surfaces and decorated china plates and jugs that were ranged attractively on shelves about the room, before he looked out of the window at the garden. 'I haven't seen your father about the place this morning. Is he out?'

'Yes, he had his breakfast early, then went into the shop to sort out a display for the sale.' She put a plate down on the table and added, 'This is ready to eat.'

'Thanks.' Daniel sat down and poured coffee for both of them. 'What's on the agenda for this morning? I'm due at Waterleys at twelve but if there's anything you want me to help out with before then, I'm all yours.'

The glimmer in his eyes looked innocent enough but Sarah's hand wavered a little all the same as she reached for a piece of toast. Having him all to herself was not something she particularly welcomed.

She spread marmalade on the toast and said evenly, 'Is there anything you'd specially like to do this morning? A trip into the village, perhaps? I could show you some of the best parts, like the old mill or the seventeenth-century inn. Or, of course, you could just relax about the house. We've plenty of books and magazines about the place and the garden's looking a treat already this year. That's Margaret's pride and joy. You—'

'There's really no need for you to feel that you have to entertain me, you know. What would you have been doing today if I wasn't staying here?'

'Well...I suppose I would have worked on the repairs I told you about yesterday,' she answered him, putting down the toast and pausing to carefully lick the smears of butter from her fingers. She flicked a quick glance at him and found that he was watching her, an oddly intent look in his blue eyes that made her feel suddenly strangely breathless.

She remembered the way it had felt to be in his arms last night—the way his hands had touched her, sliding over the thin silk of her robe. For a second or two she almost faltered, then she lowered her hands to the table once more and managed to find her voice. 'I really need to spend every spare moment on them if I'm to have the book ready in time.'

'Then that's what you must do,' Daniel said briskly. 'I'd rather like to watch you at work, if I may? Or would that bother you?'

It would probably bother her a great deal since her alarm sensors appeared to be constantly activated where he was concerned but to refuse such a simple request would only make her look foolish.

Sarah gave a light shrug. 'If that's what you

want... I'll have to leave here at about eleven to ferry the plants over to Waterleys and get them set up on the stall. As soon as I've done that I'll be free to show you around. I've a friend who will keep an eye on things for me for a while.'

'We'll go in my car,' he said. 'Your father said yours was out of action. I'll stow the trays in the boot just before we go and what we can't get in there we'll put on the back seat. I noticed you have a huge collection in the conservatory. Mostly Margaret's work, your father said. She must be a very keen gardener.'

'She is. This sort of occasion puts her in her element. There'd be no stopping her.' She sent him a quick glance. 'You must have extensive grounds at your home. Do you get to enjoy them much or are you constantly on the move? It must be an exciting kind of life to go thousands of miles to places that people like me only dream of.'

'I'm often away for months at a time,' he agreed, and she wondered fleetingly if he would be going away again soon—if that would give them some kind of reprieve.

His mouth curved as though he had read her thoughts and he said softly, 'It isn't as glamorous as you might imagine. We spend an awful lot of time living in trailers and generally roughing it. In fact, I may not go away again for some considerable time. There are other things I want to do.'

'Oh?' Sarah's throat closed on the news, and she swallowed hard on her toast. 'What kind of things? More books? I know you brought out a couple last year to go along with the TV programmes. They were very popular and I thought about buying them but they were a bit too expensive for me.'

'The hardbacks are, I'm afraid. I don't have a say in the pricing of them but I can let you have copies. I'm sure I have one or two lying around, back at the Hall.'

She was horrified, wishing that she hadn't let her tongue run away with her. 'I wasn't hinting—'

'Of course you weren't.' Daniel's mouth twisted fiendishly. 'And you wouldn't want to be beholden to me in any way, I do realise that. All the same, I shall insist that you accept them.'

She tried to cover her embarrassment by taking refuge in pouring coffee, though, catching sight of his wryly amused expression, she doubted that she had succeeded very well.

'Tell me about Margaret,' he said. 'Has she always lived here with you? She's never been married?'

'She came to stay with us when I was eight, just after my mother died. I think my father was lost for a while in his own grief and didn't quite know how to cope so Margaret stepped into the breach and organised us both. No, she never married though I'm not sure why.

'I don't know if there was anyone in her past but she's always concentrated very hard on her career; turned all her energies into that. She loves teaching. The school's like a second home to her—I think she'd live there if she could.'

'I'm sorry to hear about your mother,' Daniel said.

'You were very young and it must have been hard for all of you.'

'She was never strong, apparently. Then one winter she contracted a virus and she was gone within a week. Yes, it was a terrible shock.'

They were both silent for a while after that, both occupied with their own thoughts, until Sarah broke out of her reverie and made a move to clear the table of the breakfast things.

When she had finished she set out her equipment on the table and reached for the book of poems that she had been working on the evening before. Daniel came and sat on the edge of the table, watching her—his long body relaxed, one hand curving lightly around the bevelled pine.

'I've repaired the torn pages already,' she said, adding, because he'd shown an interest, 'We use tissue because that way the print underneath can still be seen. And I've finished working on the spine where that was damaged.

'The main problem here is that I need to re-cover the boards of the book with leather. It's been a slow process because the corners were worn away and I've had to build them up with chippings of leather and paste before I could make a start on anything else.'

'You've made a good job of it,' he remarked. 'The end result is very smooth and even.'

'It has to be if the final leather covering is to look any good.' She worked all the while she talked, pasting the rectangle of thin leather until it was supple and manageable and then carefully applying it to the boards. 'Again, the corners are the difficult part,' she told him. 'They have to be just right, very evenly finished, or the whole thing can look a mess.'

'That's what these clamps are for, is it? So that you can make sure everything stays in place while it's drying out?'

'That's right. When it's completely dry I'll work the title onto the front cover and spine. After that, all that's left to be done is to apply a few coats of furbishing cream and it will look as good as new.'

'I'm impressed,' he said, when she had finished the task. 'Where did you learn how to do this?'

'I took a course at the local poly when I'd finished my other studies. It seemed a practical thing to do if I was going to be working with my father.'

'The shop means a lot to him, doesn't it?'

'He's put a lot into it over the years.' She stared up at him. 'Though now it seems as if it was all for nothing.'

'Maybe not. He might get a buyer who's prepared to pay a good price.'

Sarah's lips firmed. 'I wasn't thinking in terms of selling up and making a profit,' she said tautly. Not that a profit seemed very likely, considering the current state of the market. It would be something if he just broke even. 'I was thinking more of the less tangible aspects of the job.'

'You were being purely sentimental. Basing your view of things on your emotions instead of using your head.'

She stood up and began to tidy away her tools. 'I

might have expected you to say something like that. You talk like a cold-blooded businessman.'

'You make it sound like a dirty word. Isn't your Philip a businessman?'

'That's different...he's different and the business he runs is not the same.' Somehow the factories didn't inspire in her the same kind of loyalty. Perhaps because they were larger, with a bigger workforce, and were less family-orientated. Anyway, they weren't under threat.

'Philip isn't likely to go along with your attitude,' she said stiffly, adding with a hint of accusation, '*He* doesn't have anything to gain from the sale of the shop.'

Daniel ignored the inflexion, asking her calmly, 'What does he do? How did you meet him?'

'He manages one of his father's textile factories and acts as troubleshooter when his father is too busy to deal with things himself. There are three factories altogether, dotted about the county.'

Sarah finished clearing up and went to wash her hands at the sink. 'We met at an exhibition a couple of summers ago. He had a stand there and I was looking for materials for the cottage—for curtains and upholstery. I thought he seemed very sensible and quiet, not at all pushy, and I liked him from the first.'

'You feel you have to defend your reasons for liking him?' His tone was idly amused and it made her sharply indignant.

'Certainly not. I can't imagine where you get that idea from and anyway I don't have to try to explain my feelings to you, of all people. I doubt if you'd understand them if I tried.'

'I think I might make a fair stab at it. In fact, I'd probably take great pleasure in finding out exactly what it is that makes you tick.' He had begun to walk slowly towards her and his complacent, very male assurance made her heart give a strange little lopsided jump.

'It's getting late,' she said hurriedly. 'It's close to eleven o'clock and we should be leaving now.'

'Should we?' His eyes held a sudden blue gleam but he only said, 'Perhaps we should postpone this discussion, then, for another time.'

'I think we've said all that needs to be said,' she answered, thankful that she was able to keep her voice steady. 'If you'd open the boot of your car I'll make a start on loading up.'

He acknowledged her cool dismissal with a dry smile and set about organising the trays of plants. Within a few minutes they had everything packed into his car and were on their way.

Waterleys was a relatively short distance away from the cottage and it wasn't long before they came up on the steep rise overlooking the open fields and thick hedgerows of the wildlife park. A series of lakes linked by a meandering river dotted the landscape, glittering like silver in the strong sunlight.

'It's going to be a scorcher today,' Daniel said, and Sarah nodded, agreeing with him, glad that she'd chosen to wear a sleeveless top and cool cotton skirt.

'Drive on past Stoneleigh House,' she instructed

him as they followed a bend in the road. 'The entrance is about half a mile further on.'

'Isn't that the Prescott-Searle place?' he asked, slowing down to peer beyond the Lodge to the white-painted house, partly hidden by the overhang of huge beech trees that lined the long, curving drive. 'What is it, eighteenth century? It looks huge.'

'It is. It's been the family home for several generations.' Sarah's lips made an odd little twist. 'There are three main storeys but over the years there have been quite a number of alterations made to the building—extensions and architectural features, and so on.'

Daniel must have picked up on something in her tone because he said questioningly, 'You don't like them?'

'I think I'd have been inclined to keep any alterations in line with the original structure. To be honest, I think it's too fussy and ornate now. It looks a bit like a square cake with icing that's been dolloped on top in lots of peaks and curves.'

He laughed softly at that. 'I shall have to take a closer look some time.'

'Lots of people like it,' she said quickly. 'Some people even consider it beautiful.'

'The Lodge looks reasonable enough. Very simple in design and fairly compact.'

'It isn't bad. Small inside, though.'

He sent her an oblique glance. 'Does anyone live there?'

She hesitated. 'Not...yet. Philip stays there

occasionally when they have guests up at the main house and he wants some privacy.'

He was thoughtful as he turned his attention back towards the road. 'Do I detect a note of reservation? Are there plans in store?'

'For the Lodge?' She made a little grimace. 'Possibly. Philip and his parents are keen for us to live there eventually once we're married.'

His gaze shifted briefly to her hands, lying restlessly in her lap. 'You're not wearing a ring,' he observed. 'Does that mean you're dispensing with an engagement?'

'We decided to wait until my birthday in a couple of months.'

'And the wedding?'

'That will be the year after, probably. In the summer, when the factories close down for the annual break.'

'How very practical.' A thin thread of mockery sounded in his voice. 'Does your Philip always think things through down to the last detail? Dot every "i" and cross every "t" even where his love life is concerned?' She felt his eyes narrow on her, darkly penetrating. 'Or is it you who's the one holding back?'

Sarah stiffened, wishing that he wouldn't look at her that way—as though he would see into her mind and read her inner thoughts.

'There's hardly any need for us to rush headlong into things,' she pointed out coolly. 'Marriage is a very important business...but you wouldn't know about that, I suppose? I dare say you've never even considered trying it. You're used to your freedom and it's far too precious a commodity to give up, isn't it?'

'Now you're definitely on the defensive. We weren't talking about me or my lifestyle. Anyway, I should hope I'd be a whole lot more enthusiastic about things if I was contemplating marriage.'

'Which you're not. Could we talk about something else, do you think?' They were approaching the main entrance to the park and she pointed out the small marina where about a dozen brightly painted canal boats were tied up.

'The car park is just over to the right. The locks mark the beginning of the trail and beyond those there are a series of lakes where all kinds of waterbirds have taken to breeding. We could walk over there later if you'd like to take a look, but first I must organise the plant stall. We're in the field where those marquees have been set up.'

'I see them.' Daniel drew the car to a halt on the rough gravel and climbed out, going around to the boot to help with the transfer of the plants.

'Philip's parents are really keen on conservation. They're hoping for a good turnout today, to boost the fund.'

'I expect they'll get it.' He seemed to have accepted her change of subject and she was relieved that they managed to work together peaceably for the next half hour or so.

She did as she had promised and showed him around, introducing him to several people on the way, until Philip and his father arrived just before twelve.

Maurice Prescott-Searle was a solidly built man with steel-grey hair and busy hazel eyes. He had a seat on the town council which suited him very well because he liked to have a hand in the way things were run. He made quick decisions and he was keen to get things moving.

He shook Daniel's hand now, and said, 'It's good to have you here, Courtenay. I've always admired your work. Can't say anyone's done more to give people an insight into the animal psyche. Brilliant. I'm enormously pleased you managed to find time to fit us in. Now, has my son discussed the matter of the fee for your appearance here today?'

As he spoke, he was ushering Daniel towards the bandstand where the formal proceedings were to take place. He took it for granted that Philip and Sarah would follow but just for a moment Sarah hesitated, smiling up into Philip's eyes. She didn't really imagine that he would kiss her, not in public, but just a light hug or squeeze would have cheered her a little.

He fell into step behind his father, taking her with him, his hand at her elbow as though he thought she might not know that they were expected to go along, too. He looked harassed.

'I've had nothing but trouble of one kind or another this morning,' he complained in a heavy undertone. 'The man who brought the donkeys over first thing has gone down with some sort of stomach complaint and we've had to send him to the first-aid tent. He'll be out of action for the rest of the day, from the looks of things. Lord knows how we're to get the animals home again. We'll have to hire someone, I suppose...unless I drive them myself.'

He appeared to be giving the matter some thought. 'I have to be over at the coast tomorrow, anyway, to sort out an offer for new machinery.'

Sarah's smile faded, though she tried her best to listen sympathetically to what he had to say. She ought not to have expected a warmer greeting. Of course he was pleased to see her; he just had other things on his mind right now.

'You're going to talk business on a Sunday?' she asked.

'It's someone my father knows,' Philip explained. 'We should be able to negotiate a good discount.'

'I could go with you,' Sarah said. 'When you've sorted out all the business of the machinery we could perhaps spend some time by the sea. I could do with a break, even a short one. Just lately it's all been a bit of a strain, with the uncertainty about the shop and everything.'

'I don't know why you worry so much about the shop. You won't be working there once we're married, anyway. We've already talked about that and you know you'll be kept busy enough entertaining our clients, acting as my hostess.'

'You mean you've talked about it,' she corrected him. 'But I don't want to argue about that now. Can't we make arrangements for tomorrow? I'd love to spend some time on a beach with you. Dad's made arrangements to go over to a friend's house so it isn't as though I'd be leaving him alone for the holiday weekend.'

'You wouldn't want to come along, Sarah. My father will be going with me and we could be talking business all day. It would be very boring for you. Why don't you go over to the house and spend the day with Mother? She's been asking you to go over fabrics and furnishings for the Lodge for some time now. She's full of ideas and interior design is her thing, you know. The sooner you sit down and discuss it with her the sooner we can make a start on the work.'

Sarah glanced at the figure of Maurice Prescott-Searle, striding ahead. He was still talking to Daniel who was glancing about him as they walked, nodding occasionally at various comments.

'But I'm not sure I want to live at the Lodge,' she said in a low voice. 'You know that. It's too small for one thing. There are only two bedrooms and one of those is minute.'

'What do we want with more? My parents have already said that any guests we have can stay at the main house and that's where we'll most likely be doing all our entertaining.'

'I wasn't thinking of guests,' she said drily.

His mouth twisted as he followed her line of thought. 'Darling, we don't want our lives cluttered up with children—not for a long while. We need time for ourselves. Surely you can see that? Besides, neither of us is from a large family and the Lodge will be perfect for what we need, you'll see.'

'I don't think—'

'Sarah, this is hardly the time or place for us to be having this conversation.'

He was right, of course. They had arrived at the bandstand where a crowd had already gathered: some of them sprawled on the grass, drinks in hand; others wandering about chatting as they enjoyed the late spring sunshine.

'Would you mind,' Philip said, turning to Daniel and his father, 'if I don't stay to listen to the speeches? I really ought to go and find out what's happening with the catering. I don't think they've ordered enough soft rolls.'

Neither of the men seemed to have any objection and he told Sarah, 'We'll talk later, darling. Do me a favour, will you, and go over and see to the donkeys for me? With that man out of action we'll have to get them organised ourselves. I've left someone in charge for the moment but he has to be somewhere else in less than an hour.'

'Donkeys?' she echoed. 'You want me to see to the donkeys?'

'Keep an eye on them so that they don't wander off. And make sure the children stay put in the saddles,' he added as an afterthought. 'We're insured but I'd rather we didn't have any accidents.'

Her skin paled a little. 'But I don't know anything about donkeys,' she protested. 'What—?'

'There's nothing to it,' he said, with a hint of impatience. 'You'll manage. You'll be fine.'

'But what about food. . .and water? When do they eat? What. . .how long—?'

He had already turned away, though, walking

briskly towards the refreshment tent, and she began to worry at her lip with her teeth, knowing that her anxious questions were falling on deaf ears.

'Problems?' Daniel asked, throwing her a searching look. 'Maybe I could help?'

'You?' Maurice put in. 'But you're doing enough already—we couldn't ask—'

'You aren't asking,' Daniel said. 'I'm offering. Though I admit I do have a certain vested interest. We could do a deal, if you like. I'll waive my fee for appearing here and I'll help Sarah with the animals as soon as I've done my stint—'

'You'd do that?' Sarah said, a small wave of relief beginning to sweep over her.

'That depends on you. I did say I had a vested interest—which means there's a condition attached.'

She looked at him warily. 'What condition?'

'I'm taking part in a rally tomorrow,' he explained. 'A vintage car rally, and I need a navigator. My sister was to have done it but her five-year-old daughter has gone down with chickenpox and I was going to have to manage by myself. If you're free tomorrow, you could take her place.'

'Had you made plans for tomorrow?' Maurice asked. 'I know Philip will be busy then...'

It was clear from his expression that he thought that this was the solution to all their problems, though the fact of her having to deal with a dozen or so obstinate and wilful donkeys probably wouldn't feature very high on his list of priorities. It was the matter of the cheque that would be occupying Maurice's thoughts.

Still, it was a tempting offer... Her last contact with a donkey had been at the seaside when she was about seven and that wasn't a memory she particularly relished, since the animal had definitely had a mind of its own... And she *was* at something of a loose end tomorrow. She'd never ridden in a vintage car and it could turn out to be something of a novel experience.

'It does sound like a fair exchange,' Sarah murmured. 'I can't see any reason why not.'

'Does that mean you'll do it?' Daniel asked, a quizzical look in his eyes. 'Is it a deal?'

'A deal,' she agreed, and was startled when a faint cheer went up from the people sitting around them. She stared about her in surprise at the crowd that had grown tenfold since Daniel had appeared on the scene, and pink colour rose in her cheeks.

She hadn't realised that anyone had been listening to their conversation but now Daniel said in amusement, 'There, I have witnesses. I shall keep you to that,' and she immediately hoped that she wasn't letting herself in for something she might come to regret later.

Daniel climbed up onto the bandstand and declared the proceedings open. He made a short but humorous speech that put the assembly in a good mood and introduced the group of musicians who were to provide ongoing entertainment before stepping down. He'd been booked to judge various competitions at intervals during the afternoon but Sarah was getting to know him well enough by now to know that he'd fit them all in somehow. If he'd made up his mind to help her, then help her he would.

Maurice went off in search of his wife, who had been overseeing operations in the crafts tent for the major part of the morning, and Sarah sent a vaguely anxious glance towards the donkeys' pasture. There was no sign of the man who was supposed to be watching over them.

'Don't you feel comfortable around animals?' Daniel asked, following the direction of her gaze.

'I can't say that I'm really used to them,' she told him. 'Apart from pets, that is. I get along fairly well with small things. There were a few about the place when I was a child, rabbits and guinea pigs and cats and so on, but I don't remember any of them ever being much above a foot high.'

He chuckled and it was a warm, throaty sound, pleasing on the ear—except that Sarah didn't think that the predicament Philip had left her in was at all funny. Her glance went to the dozen or so animals waiting in a straggly circle at the far end of the field and her brows pulled together in a frown. 'Shouldn't they be roped together or something?'

'Come on,' he said, taking her hand firmly in his. 'We'll go over there and see if, between us, we can muddle through somehow.'

His hand engulfed her smaller one. It was warm and strong and infinitely capable and somehow that simple action helped give her a feeling of total security and well-being. Daniel was a man you could put your trust in; the thought tumbled across her mind as he led her away. A man who wouldn't let you down.

She shook her head a little to clear the strange images that were crowding in. Trust him? What was she thinking of? There were some aspects to his character that should definitely be treated with a measure of caution. For a start, he'd probably had more women friends than she'd had hot breakfasts. No, letting her guard down around him was a dangerous thing to do; the sort of reckless act only a woman who was completely off her head would even begin to contemplate.

Still, he *was* good with the animals; she had to admit that. He had them rounded up in no time and the children who were clamouring for rides laughed gleefully as he lifted them up into the saddles. Even the timid ones managed a shy smile as he coaxed them to pat the donkeys' flanks and she could see their confidence slowly grow as he talked to them.

When they had plucked up enough courage to actually ride he walked along with them, his hand firm on the pommel, showing them that there was nothing to fear.

'I don't know how I'd have coped without you,' Sarah told him as they called a halt later on in the afternoon. He'd dealt with the competitions and organised the drawing of the raffle, and now people were beginning to pack up their stalls. She'd managed to slip away, though, and bring back a couple of cans of cold drinks from the beer tent before it, too, shut down. She had a raging thirst and she was sure that Daniel must be feeling the same.

He finished putting out buckets of feed for the animals and filled a trough with fresh water before he straightened up and accepted the can that she held out to him.

'Thanks.' He tugged the ring-pull and took a long swallow. 'Lord, I needed that. It hasn't been this hot all year. What do you say we go and sit over by the weir for a while? I think we deserve a break, don't you?'

They left the donkeys safely tethered and walked over to a quietly secluded place where willows shaded the grass by the weir and the water rippled clear and bright over the brown rocks, breaking into iridescent bubbles of white foam as it met the river below.

They sat down and Sarah eased the sandals from her feet, enjoying the tickle of sun-warmed grass on her bare legs.

'This is the life,' she said with a sigh. 'Nothing to do but lie back and while away the hours. There's nothing to compare with the tranquillity of the English countryside, is there? It's so green and peaceful that it always makes me feel good.' She pulled at a blade of grass, running it lightly between her fingers. 'Still, you've travelled all over, haven't you? I expect there are places you'd far rather be.'

Daniel's gaze drifted slowly over her. 'I wouldn't say that,' he murmured. He didn't say any more and Sarah felt more hot than ever and decided that it might be wise to change the subject.

'You did a great job this afternoon,' she said. 'You were a real hit with the crowd and the children loved you. Are you used to youngsters? I know you said you had a niece and you certainly seemed very much at ease with them.'

'I've a fair number of young relatives. I like having them around, I must admit. They always seem so full of life and enthusiasm for everything and they soak up knowledge like sponges.'

'So, do you think you might call in one day at Aunt Margaret's school?'

'I'll talk to her about it if she phones.'

'Oh, I'm sure she will.' Her voice drifted languidly away. It was much too hot and everything was becoming far too much of an effort.

Stretching luxuriously, Sarah lifted a hand to draw the soft weight of her hair from her nape and allow a gentle waft of air to cool her heated skin.

'I really should have tied this up,' she murmured lazily, tilting her head back and closing her eyes against the dazzling rays of the sun. She felt its warm, red glow on her eyelids. 'Or put it up, or something. I'd forgotten quite how hot it can make me feel. Maybe I should get it cut before the summer.'

She felt, rather than heard, him move and knew that his long body had shifted beside her until he was shading out the sun. When she opened her eyes a fraction she found that he was studying her, tracing her features one by one, his gaze lingering on the bright sheen of her shoulder-length hair.

'Don't do that,' he said. 'Your hair is beautiful and it would be a crying shame to have it lopped off when a few pins would serve the same purpose.'

Slowly he reached for her, sliding his hands behind her head to scoop up the silky, chestnut waves and a tremor of startled reaction ran through her limbs. She couldn't read his expression but his eyes were every bit as hot and blue as the sky.

She was mesmerised by that vivid, shimmering look or she might have resisted the warm glide of his fingers at the back of her neck. Instead a pulse of heat intensified inside her at his touch—a ripple of unexpected pleasure shooting through every nerve fibre of her being, leaving a sweet, drowsy intoxication in its wake.

'Does that feel better?' he asked.

His voice was soft and low and as he spoke his hands were moving gently, seductively, over her skin, his thumb feathering a path along the slender, sensitised curve of her throat so that she forgot the question and could only think how close he was, how subtle was the fragrance of cologne that drifted lightly on the air between them and how much she hoped that the gentle caress of his fingers on her skin would go on and on.

It was a drugging sensation: the stroking of his hands on her body; the warmth of his hand on her back irrevocably pressing her close to him. His head bent towards her until his mouth was just a heartbeat away and even as she realised that he meant to kiss her she knew that she could not draw back. When it came she felt the brush of his lips on hers like a fierce shock of heat; a vibrant, tingling explosion of sensation that shook her to the core.

Daniel took possession of her mouth with slow

deliberation, exploring the softness of her lips with a thoroughness that brought a peculiar weakness to her limbs and made her glad she was sitting down otherwise she was sure that her legs would have crumpled beneath her. Sarah's fingers spread across the broad sweep of his shoulders and it was an unaccustomed feeling to discover the taut stretch of muscle beneath his shirt. It helped to bring her to her senses; that encounter with unfamiliar hard male strength acting like a shower of cool water to clear some of the haziness from her mind.

How could she have behaved so irresponsibly? She had never imagined that a kiss could be like that—that it could make her feel so alive, so achingly, wildly responsive. And at the same time so treacherously disloyal.

She pushed him away, acknowledging the surprised flex of muscle beneath her fingers, and then pushed harder. His eyes had been half-closed as he kissed her and now he opened them, staring down at her, the heat in them still flickering like the glowing embers of a fire. His hands curved around her arms.

'Sarah—'

'Don't,' she said huskily, shaking her head. 'I don't want this. I should never have let you kiss me. I don't know why it happened.'

'I could hazard a guess. Do you want me to spell it out?'

'No! I behaved stupidly. I know that well enough; I don't need the message rammed home.' She shook herself free of his hands and started to get to her feet, looking around for her sandals and smoothing down the material of her skirt with fingers that trembled. 'I'm practically engaged to Philip.'

Daniel stood up, towering above her as she awkwardly pushed her toes into her shoes. '*Practically* is hardly the same as *actually*,' he pointed out drily.

'Maybe not, but it feels the same to me,' she flared. 'I should be with him now, not spending time here with you.'

'Go to him, then. Run away if that's what you want.' His mouth took on an odd, cynical slant. 'Just don't expect me to say I'm sorry, will you? I'd be a liar if I did that.'

'I don't expect anything of you,' she said, an edge of bitterness creeping into her voice. 'I should have followed my instincts and kept well away from you. I knew the minute you came into the shop that you were trouble.'

'But you didn't keep away,' he reminded her crisply. 'And I'm involved with you and your family, one way and another, whether you like it or not. I'm not going to go away and fade conveniently out of your life because it suits you better that way. I'm here, and I'll be here as long as I have dealings with your father. Remember that when you partner me tomorrow.'

She felt the colour draining away from her face. 'Tomorrow? You wouldn't still keep me to that?'

'Wouldn't I? You don't know me very well yet, do you, Sarah? Or you'd know that I always carry through whatever I've started, right to the end.'

CHAPTER FIVE

DANIEL called for Sarah at ten the next day, looking fresh and relaxed in an open-necked shirt and finely tailored dark trousers—as though he'd had just a few minutes' drive instead of a two-hour journey along the motorway.

Sarah refused to feel guilty because she had turned down the invitation he'd put to her to go with him to his home last night. It might have saved him a lot of to-ing and fro-ing, but that was his hard luck. He knew full well that she'd had second thoughts about this rally but he wasn't backing down.

Last night she'd been thoroughly agitated, filled with doubts. Why had she let him kiss her? It must have been the heat of the day, the aftermath of a busy afternoon, when her defences were at their lowest ebb. That must be the reason. She had never even thought about being with another man since she'd known Philip.

Sarah wished that she could have gone with Philip to the coast. It hadn't mattered to her that he would be talking business with his father much of the time. She just needed to be with him, to be reassured by his calming presence. She had seen precious little of him just lately as it was.

'Darling, I know it's a nuisance,' he'd said, when she'd pressed him to change his mind, 'but I can't let my father down, and it *is* going to be purely a business meeting. You know how involved he gets when he's decided on something. It's only for one day—not even as much as that. I'll be back in the evening and we'll go out somewhere, just the two of us.'

So she'd kissed him goodbye and gone back to the cottage to work on the book repairs for a few hours. At least her time had been usefully filled.

'Did you have a good journey?' she enquired now of Daniel, more out of politeness than from any real desire to know. He wasn't giving any consideration to her feelings in this and she didn't see why she should put herself out any more than was necessary. She was only doing this at all for her father's sake.

He could call in the loan, he'd said, and, despite her reservations, she didn't want to antagonise Daniel Courtenay unduly. She didn't think that he'd go back on the arrangements he'd made with her father but she wasn't about to put it to the test. Her father was worried enough as it was and if Daniel did call in the loan they stood to lose the cottage as well as the shop.

'I did, thanks. The holiday traffic seems to have fallen off.' His gaze ranged over her, coming to linger on the smoothly pinned french pleat of her hair. 'You're looking very cool and poised,' he said. 'The heat won't be getting to you today, will it?'

There was a devilish slant to his jaw and a fitful gleam in his eye that told her he knew exactly why she'd put it up out of the way. The weather had nothing to do with it. He'd said he liked it down and it was purely that which had prompted her to pin it up.

Sarah hadn't known what she ought to wear today. What *did* people wear for rallies of this sort? Ordinary everyday clothes or something more in keeping with the era? In the end she'd opted for a calf-length jade skirt and a white, pin-tucked blouse that was buttoned up to the throat. A pair of slender-fitting, ankle-high black boots completed the outfit.

'It does look as though it's going to be another fine day, doesn't it? More of a breeze than yesterday, though,' she answered him, reaching for the bag that she had left on the coffee table.

Daniel opened the door. 'Shall we go?'

'Tell me about the rally,' she said, once she was settled into his car and they were heading along the road to the south.

'It's just a holiday run along the country roads. There are various stops along the way where we check clues that will tell us where we should be headed. We motor along, enjoying the fresh air and sunshine, and meet up somewhere later. Usually a pub.'

'Do you belong to a club of some sort? How long have you been interested in vintage cars?'

'For as long as I can remember,' he told her. 'Yes, I do belong to a club. My grandfather was a keen collector of vintage cars and I suppose a lot of his interest rubbed off on me. He was forever tinkering and polishing and I was always fascinated by the cars he kept in the carriage block behind the Hall. When

I was just a boy he used to take me with him to auctions and collections dotted about the country.'

'Used to?'

'He died a long time ago, unfortunately. He was a good man; chirpy as a sparrow, as I remember him.'

'It sounds as though you were very fond of him.'

'I was.'

'Are you a close-knit family? You mentioned your sister would have been with you today.'

'I'd say we are, yes. My sister, Claire, lives with her husband in a house just outside London so that he can commute to the City fairly easily. He's a banker. They've two children, a boy and a girl, who keep Claire on her toes but she still manages to do some part-time work for a charity organisation.

'Adam, my younger brother, is a whizkid on the Stock Exchange. He isn't married. He has a bachelor apartment in London and, from what I gather, he's enjoying life too much at the moment to want to settle down.'

That was something the two brothers clearly had in common, Sarah thought drily, though she kept her opinion strictly to herself. She'd read enough about Daniel Courtenay to know that he'd had a number of glamorous and possessive female companions over the years but there had never been any sign of his wanting to tie the knot.

Daniel wanted to know about her own family but there was only her father and Aunt Margaret and by comparison it seemed a lonely little world. She told him about her childhood days, spent exploring the village of Wellbrook and the surrounding countryside with friends she grew up with.

They reached his home in what seemed like no time at all and Sarah's eyes widened in stunned surprise as he turned the car into a wide, curving drive. She wasn't sure quite what she had expected. Certainly not this elegant, stone-built mansion, the sun's rays casting it in golden light so that it appeared to glow like a bright jewel set in the heart of wooded, green countryside.

She pulled in a sharp breath. '*This* is your home?' she said thickly. 'It's so beautiful. I think it's the loveliest house I've ever seen.'

'I'm glad you like it,' he murmured, switching off the engine and turning to face her. 'We've always been fond of the place.'

'Is it the family home? I mean, is it your mother's house?'

'It actually belongs to me. The peculiar inheritance processes we have to go through mean that the property passes to the eldest son but of course it will always remain my mother's home as long as she wants to stay here.

'She has her own suite of rooms but I think, now that my father is no longer with us, she'll prefer to spend most of her time at their other house in Kent. It's smaller and she says she feels more comfortable there, with friends she's known for years. It's also nearer to Adam and Claire.'

Sarah's brow creased into a small frown. 'How do Adam and Claire feel about you inheriting the place?'

Daniel gave her a brief, faint smile. 'There's no animosity, if that's what you're thinking. They were left well provided for and they've always known how things would be. We all get on remarkably well.'

He climbed out of the car and came to hold open the door for her. 'Let me show you around. We've half an hour or so before we need to be making tracks—time enough for a drink on the terrace. I thought we'd have a proper lunch later but you'll probably appreciate a snack now. I'll get Annie, my housekeeper, to fix us something.'

Daniel helped her from the car and led her towards the front entrance, his hand sliding casually around her waist as they walked—but there was nothing casual in the way her body responded to that light touch.

The instant she felt his palm flatten on her rib cage in warm possessiveness, gently nudging the rounded swell of her hip, her nerves leapt like guttering flames. She wondered dazedly whether the searing imprint of his fingers might lie like a burn on her skin for ever.

It alarmed her terribly, feeling this way. She couldn't want this. How could she? She loved Philip. She wished he could be here now to restore her sense of balance, to help keep her feet firmly on the ground.

It was silly to be disturbed by such a simple act. It was a natural gesture, as casual as shaking hands, but she pulled away all the same, walking a little apart from him with her blue-grey eyes fixed determinedly on the impressive porticoed entrance to the Hall.

'It looks as though it has stood here for centuries,' Sarah said quickly. 'How far back does it go?'

Daniel's mouth made a wry shape as though he knew just how desperately she had needed to put a distance between them but he only said, 'The original building dates back to 1450, though there have been several spates of alteration and extension since then. The east wing was added around 1820 and the library was renovated about ten years ago, still in keeping with the whole feel of the place, of course.'

He took her through to the hall, where a grand curving staircase rose to the balconied upper floor. At its base, set on an ornately carved antique table, was a huge flower arrangement, its delicate fragrance filling the air. There were gladioli, irises and orchids and Sarah couldn't resist stopping to gently touch the waxy petals of a pink bloom and breathe in its scent.

'They're brought in from the gardens and glasshouses,' Daniel explained. 'Margaret and my gardener, Ben, would get on a treat.'

'I'm sure they would. Your gardens must be spectacular if these flowers are anything to go by.'

'I enjoy them when I'm here. I'll give you a whirlwind tour of the house,' he said. 'Just bear with me while I find Annie.'

The house lived up to the promise of its splendid exterior, with panelled rooms and huge fireplaces and latticed windows looking out over sweeping lawns and landscaped grounds. All the furniture was richly antique, highly polished and exquisitely upholstered.

It *was* a whirlwind tour, as he'd said, just of the ground floor to begin with because Annie found them after a few minutes to say that coffee was ready and anyway they were to set off in a short while to meet up with the other members of the club.

'I can't take it all in,' Sarah said faintly. 'I'd just no idea what to expect.'

He showed her out onto the paved terrace, where a table had been laid with iced drinks and freshly made sandwiches cut into tempting squares. There was a plate of little cakes and a tray set for coffee, with pristine white napkins folded into long glasses. When they were seated by the stone balustrade, Daniel poured juice for both of them.

'You must love coming back here,' Sarah murmured, looking about her at the broad sweep of rolling lawn that sloped down to a smooth lake edged by reeds and shaded by the gentle overhang of trees.

'I do.' He handed her a plate, pushing the sandwiches towards her, and grinned—a lopsided affair that made him appear even more attractive than ever. 'It certainly beats mud huts and termites any time.'

'You've stayed in some inhospitable places, haven't you?' she said, taking some of the food he offered and sampling it appreciatively.

'I remember watching a film you made near an African village. It looked so primitive. Later on you were shown standing near a group of lions and you seemed to be so close to them I kept wondering what you were feeling at the time. You didn't look as though it bothered you at all. Haven't you ever been afraid?'

Daniel considered the question for a moment. 'You need to observe a certain amount of elementary caution at all times, though there's usually someone ready nearby in case sudden problems crop up. I didn't really think the lions would be particularly troublesome since they'd just had a good meal.'

His mouth twisted a little as he reached for a sandwich. 'If we're talking real fear, though...my grandmother was a different kettle of fish altogether. She could freeze me on the spot with just a look, never mind what she had to say..."It's high time you settled down, Daniel, my boy"..."When are you going to stop gallivanting around the world like a demented grasshopper? You'll give your poor mother a heart attack before you've finished."'

His imitation of a frosty matriarch made Sarah smile but she asked softly, 'Has she gone, too?'

'Afraid so. She was a strong woman but even the strongest have to go some time.'

'Was that her portrait I saw in the hall?' Sarah recalled a rather austere lady who looked as though she was keeping firm control on all that went on around her. Her expression was cool and unsmiling and Sarah could see why anyone might be in awe of her, though she suspected Daniel was only joking about how he had felt.

'That's the one. Perhaps I'll have her moved. She

does tend to dominate the scene, even though she's no longer around.'

'Would she have approved of this afternoon's outing?' She sipped slowly at the fruit juice.

'Oh, I'm sure she would. She was always keen to get out and about and the Rolls often had an airing, but the pub lunch would have been strictly off limits. My grandfather's liking for the odd tipple was definitely frowned on.'

'The Rolls? Is it still around? Is it part of the collection?'

'It is. There's a 1905 Stanhope Phaeton and a little donkey carriage that my great-grandmother used to ride about in. We ought to have had that with us yesterday. There's also a 1930 Mercedes-Benz, but the Rolls is my pride and joy. It's a 1907 Silver Ghost that my grandfather bought and renovated in the twenties. We'll be going out in that.'

A few minutes later, when they had finished making inroads into the food, they walked around the house to the carriage block where the car was kept in readiness.

Sarah eyed its gleaming coachwork and roomy, open-topped interior and said in awed tones, 'I can see why this is your favourite. It's sumptuous. It will seem almost criminal to take it out and get it dusty.'

Daniel chuckled softly. 'We shan't worry about that. Climb in and we'll head for the open road.'

When she was settled in the passenger seat, he pushed a map into her hands. 'We'll be going towards Highbridge,' he told her, 'following the country lanes by Rolston Farm and on towards the reservoir.'

She spread the map open on her knee and consulted it, trying to get her bearings while he started up the car and manoeuvred it out on to the main drive. 'You asked me to navigate for you,' she said, 'but you didn't ask if I was any good at it. Aren't you afraid I might get us lost?'

He flicked her a sidelong glance, a faint gleam sparkling in the depths of his blue eyes.

'That's a chance I'll have to take. I doubt if I'll be too worried, though. In fact, it might turn out to be a very agreeable experience, all things considered... because if we do get separated from the others and finish up stranded, miles out of our way, we can always find a cosy hotel that will put us up for the night. I don't see that as a problem. Do you?'

His tone was wickedly mocking and she stared at him in shocked dismay, her mind following the path of his thoughts and coming to a feverish pass. Spend the night with him? His words were teasing but she knew full well that the thread of promise in them was real enough. He had never made any secret of the fact that he wanted her. She could read every signal, every nuance of every gesture.

Her heart began to race wildly, setting up a primitive beat all of its own, the pulse at her throat hammering in unison. It was just the kind of fiendishly provocative suggestion that she might have expected him to come up with, but there was no way she would ever risk such a thing. A night with Daniel Courtenay? Her life would never be the same again.

Sarah took a deep breath and said firmly, 'I most certainly do so you can forget that idea straight away. It simply isn't going to happen. I'm really very good at reading maps, you see. I've done it for my father for years.'

'Shame.' Daniel's jaw moved in a rakish way, giving his dangerous good looks even more of an edge and setting her blood racing all over again. 'I was beginning to quite relish the prospect of spending time with you. Champagne and candlelight, soft music. . .'

'Pure fantasy,' she said, as crisply as she could manage. 'I think you should concentrate on your driving instead of letting your mind wander into dreamland. I already have a man in my life and even if I didn't I wouldn't be fool enough to date someone like you.'

'Someone like me?' They were on the open road now and other vintage-car drivers were appearing at intervals along the way. Daniel raised a hand in acknowledgement; horns were sounded in greeting and scarves were waved. 'What's that supposed to mean?'

'Perhaps your grandmother had a point,' she muttered. 'You're not the settling kind. From all accounts, you don't stay anywhere long enough to form any lasting relationships. You kiss and move on. A woman would have to be out of her mind to pin her hopes on anything more with you.'

'You think so?' There was a trace of bitterness in his voice as he said, 'A few have been more than happy to milk what they could while the going was good.'

'Money, you mean? I dare say that works both ways. You seem to have everything else in life that money can buy. Why should a woman be any exception?'

'Why indeed?' Daniel murmured softly, turning his gaze full on her. 'Does that apply to you, too, Sarah? Do you have a price? Maybe I'm ready to listen.'

Hot colour winged its way across her cheekbones. 'That was a downright insulting question,' she said through her teeth. 'And you should be watching the road, not fixing your attention on me that way.'

She didn't like the way he studied her—as though his dark glance could penetrate every facet of her thoughts. If he read her mind and saw how confused he made her feel, she'd have no chance against him. 'I already told you I'm not up for grabs. You're wasting your time. I'm very happy with Philip.'

'Are you?' He made a scornful sound in his throat. 'If you keep telling yourself that often enough, you might even come to believe it.'

'What do you know about anything?' she retorted, stung. 'He's a good man; he's thoughtful and conscientious about everything he does.'

'Sure he is. That's why he's working on a bank holiday when he could be with the woman who's supposed to be marrying him someday. He's a cold fish, your Philip, and lord only knows why you chose him. Perhaps you're frightened of your own sexuality. Is that it, Sarah?

'Are you afraid of what might happen if a man fanned that sleeping fire? Do you think you might both be burned in the blaze? You've lived in a cloistered world, haven't you, with your aunt and your father, locked away in that quiet little bookshop...? I bet Philip is your first real man friend. What would—?'

'I don't want to hear any more of your questions and suppositions,' she cut in brusquely.

'I'm not a specimen on a microscope slide, nor am I one of your animal psycho-studies. Why don't you just concentrate on your driving instead? That's what we're here for, isn't it? That's what you said—to motor along and enjoy the fresh air. That doesn't mean I have to sit and listen to your impossible conjectures. Just get on with the business in hand, will you?'

'Now you sound like my grandmother,' he said. 'I'm beginning to quake in my boots.'

'Oh, shut up!'

Daniel's soft laughter did nothing to soothe Sarah's temper. It was only after they had stopped at various clue points along the way and applied their minds to solving the riddle of the next stage in the journey that her cool composure began to return. It was a beautiful day, as he pointed out; the birds were singing and there was only the slightest breeze to riffle through the escaping tendrils of hair at her temples. It was far too pleasant an afternoon to spend it arguing.

They arrived at the country inn about an hour later, pulling into the large car park where a few of the club members had already parked. Sarah didn't know the models of the cars assembled there but she was fascinated enough to ask and Daniel knew them all.

He introduced her to his friends, who all seemed to have come along with wives or girlfriends or family. They were a friendly crowd, taking their drinks outside at wooden tables and swapping stories of spare parts and calamities and last-minute hitches, all with good humour.

'Are you hungry?' Daniel asked, after they'd been there some time and she nodded, surprised to find that she was—though it was getting on for mid-afternoon and it had been a while since their sandwich snack.

'I think I am. Do they do meals here?' She looked around. 'I haven't noticed anyone eating but perhaps they do them inside. I'd have thought they'd have finished serving by now.'

'They do. They have. But don't worry, I have it all in hand. Let's get back to the car and we'll drive on a bit.'

Sarah did as he suggested, wondering where they were headed, and when he at last turned down an isolated, dusty road a little frown worked its way into her brow.

'I don't see anywhere,' she said.

'Just beyond those trees,' he murmured. 'There's a beautiful, serene little place by the river. Fishermen don't usually come here because it's not a good fishing spot but it should make an ideal setting for a picnic.'

'A picnic? Is that what's in the box at the back of the car?'

'You guessed it.' Daniel smiled, drawing the car to a halt and getting down to show her the way. 'Annie's a very good cook. She always prepares the food for the family when we go out anywhere—and there's always something absolutely mouth-watering.'

He wasn't exaggerating. He laid out a huge cloth on the ground and spread out such an assortment of delicacies that Sarah didn't know where to start. There was seafood in a creamy sauce—packed in ice to keep it fresh—pâté and appetising hors d'oeuvres, succulent chicken and salmon en croûte, with strawberries and ice cream to follow—all washed down with a chilled wine. She nibbled at delicious titbits and sipped slowly at the wine.

'I hope you're paying Annie plenty,' Sarah said. 'Someone who cooks like this is a treasure you can't want to lose. I feel as though I've gone to heaven and I'm sampling paradise.' Replete, she smiled at him, kicking off her boots and curling her toes into the blanket he had provided. She leaned back against plump cushions produced from the back seat of the car.

'I think,' Daniel said, watching her, 'that's the first time you've really smiled at me. I like it. You should do it more often.'

'Should I?' she queried lazily. 'I feel like smiling. It must be the wine. Perhaps I've had too much to drink on top of the glass or two I had at the pub. It's a good thing I'm not driving. It's a lovely, floaty feeling. Have you got a clear head?'

'I have a very clear head,' he murmured, his mouth creasing in a way that held her attention. He had a very attractive mouth. She stared, frowning a little at that thought for a second or two before it dissolved into mist.

'I'm glad,' she said. 'One of us needs to get us safely home again.'

'There's no need to worry about that,' he said. He was leaning too, stretched out on his side with his head resting on one elbow as he looked at her. With his free hand he picked up a pebble that had lodged in the grass and tossed it into the river. It fell with a faint splash, making ripples in the clear water. 'Have you enjoyed yourself today? You looked as though you were pleased to meet my friends.'

'I have. I've never ridden in such a grand car before or stuffed myself so full of wonderful food.' She patted her stomach. 'Much more of this and I shall need to go on a diet.' She laughed softly, then, because that was something Aunt Margaret had always sighed over. She never put on weight.

'I loved your friends,' she said. 'They were such a cheerful bunch and the women treated me as though they had known me for years. I wonder where some of them found those long, wonderful dresses? They looked just right for the occasion. Perhaps they hired them for the day. I feel as though I ought to have been wearing ankle-length skirts and a wide-brimmed hat.'

'You look perfect as you are. Like a genteel Edwardian lady out for an afternoon's drive.'

There was a faint hint of amusement in his tone and she looked at him and said guardedly, 'I'm glad you approve...I think.'

'Oh, I do, believe me. But, then, I've always thought you looked good whatever the occasion. Especially the other evening—that thin nightshirt you were nearly wearing was really something. Sent my blood pressure sky high.'

Heat curled inside her and her mouth went suddenly dry. She had thought—hoped—that he hadn't been fully aware of her state of undress, but now she could see what a futile hope that had been. This man missed absolutely nothing.

'I didn't expect to see you there,' Sarah said quickly. 'I was worried about my father and I didn't think, that's all. If I'd known you were going to be waylaying me on the stairs I'd have—'

'You'd have buttoned yourself right up to the chin, much as you have done today. Not that it makes any difference, you know.' Daniel's blue eyes made a shimmering, sensual sweep of her body, leisurely absorbing every detail of her appearance so that she was breathlessly conscious of his scrutiny, her skin burning as though he had run his hands intimately over every inch of her.

'There's something inherently tantalising about buttons,' he murmured huskily, moving closer to her and reaching out to touch the fastenings of her blouse—slowly, lingeringly, one by one. 'They were made to be undone.'

'Don't you dare,' she muttered abstractedly, heat racing through her veins, her body shaking with the intensity of her response to the warm brush of his hands on the soft swell of her breasts. The awful truth was, even as she denied it, that she *wanted* to feel his hands on her. Desire was breaking over her in waves, rushing through the walls of her defences and threatening to drown out any last vestige of common sense she had left.

'I wish... I want you, Sarah; you know that, don't you? I want to make love to you, out here on the grass with the blue sky as our ceiling and the river making music for us. I want to see you, all of you, I want to taste you, feel the silkiness of your skin against my mouth.'

Daniel leaned over her, his long body gently pressing her into the softness of the blanket and the heaped cushions, and his head bent towards her, his mouth coming down on hers, moving sensuously against the fullness of her lips.

A melting sweetness flowed through her veins and her body became pliant beneath him, moulding itself to the hot intimacy of his thighs, her hands registering the whipcord strength of the muscles in his arms and back. His tongue traced a flickering path over the ripe swell of her lips, leaving a trail of fire in its wake.

Sarah didn't know how long it was before the kiss deepened, before she lost herself completely in that sensual assault. She only knew that this was something she had craved all her life without knowing what it was she had gone without.

It was crazy—the way she responded to him, the way her body flamed and shuddered with reckless excitement at his lightest touch as though his hands belonged on her body and she was being compelled towards him, urged on by some wild, seductive passion that was running rapidly out of control.

The flimsy material of her blouse fell apart beneath the warm glide of his hands and she trembled violently as his fingers brushed the creamy slopes of her breasts. She was on fire, burning with a need that she had never known before.

She had never felt this way with Philip. What she felt for him was a quiet thing like a smooth body of water where gentle ripples barely marred the surface. It had always been enough up to now. Philip believed that they should wait until they were married before they went to bed together and she had always gone along with that. She had felt no great urgency.

Now, guilt washed over her. How could she do this to Philip? How could she be lying here with this man—who only wanted to assuage a momentary passion, who had no deep, lasting feeling for her?

His mouth was making its own sensual detour, gliding downwards along the smooth column of her throat and lingering in the warm hollow at its base. She trembled against him, her treacherous body yielding to sweet sensation as his lips drifted lower and began to trace the soft, full curve of her breast. A sob broke in her throat as she tried to deny what was happening to her.

'No,' she groaned, her voice a muffled sound

against his dark head. 'This is so wrong. Leave me alone.'

She was behaving so badly that she had to do something, and quickly, or he would move in on her sure as night crept up on day, swallowing it whole. It was what he did; was how he went through life, gathering up women along the way for his own amusement. He didn't care that there was someone else in her life. He had no scruples about breaking up her relationship with Philip.

Daniel's head lifted and he looked at Sarah, his dark eyes still smouldering with heated desire. 'You can't mean that,' he muttered, his voice roughened. 'I can feel the heat in you, the race of your heart against mine. You're so lovely, Sarah, so beautiful...'

'I love Philip,' she said, shakily. 'I love him. What kind of man are you? Is this what you had in mind all along when you asked me to come here today? A little seduction, a quick flirtation to while away a few hours? I would never have agreed to come with you if I'd known this was how it was going to be.'

The desire drained slowly out of his face. 'You make it sound as though I'm working to some kind of master plan.'

'Aren't you?'

'No.' His features were harsh now, the sun shaded out of them, his eyes chips of flint. 'But you're fooling yourself if you imagine I can't feel the way you respond to me. It isn't a one-way thing that's going on here no matter how much you protest about your relationship with your precious Philip. If that's so strong why are you so much on the defensive about it?

'What kind of marriage are you going to have if every time he takes you to bed you're thinking of how it might be with another man?'

She gasped at that, her hand shooting out in swift, involuntary reaction, but his hand caught her wrist in a steely grasp and held it in frozen motion before it could make contact with the hard-boned angles of his face.

'I wouldn't advise you to strike me,' he said raspingly. 'I fight back and you wouldn't like my tactics very much.'

Daniel's eyes clashed with hers, challenging her, and Sarah blinked, resisting the impulse to turn away from that vivid blue glance and the burning impact it had on her senses.

'I don't imagine I would,' she said, her tone clipped, the breath so tight in her lungs that it made her chest ache with strain. 'I don't think I like anything about you at all. I wish I'd never met you. I hope I never set eyes on you again after today.'

'That's because you're a coward,' he said, releasing her clamped wrist in a sudden jerky movement. 'You're afraid to take life by the throat and wring out of it what you really want. You're so afraid of hurting other people that you're hurting yourself.'

'Why should I listen to you?' she bit out. 'What do you know? You come on the scene and within five minutes you think you know everything. Well, you don't and I won't have you disrupting my life.

Just take me home. I want to get out of here. I want to get away from this place, away from you.'

'Of course. I'm hardly likely to leave you stranded, am I?' He stood up, sending a raking glance over her so that only then did she realise how dishevelled she must look with the pins coming out of her hair and silky wisps of hair escaping to fall about her face and neck.

A tremor crept over her mouth as she ran her shaking fingers over the open edges of her blouse and tried to pull them together over the skimpy lace of her bra.

He watched her movements, his mouth making a sardonic curve, and when he spoke again his voice was dipped in ice.

'Yes. It would be a good idea to get dressed first. If you go back to the car looking like that, people might think you've been making love...wild, abandoned, reckless love...and that wouldn't do at all, would it?'

CHAPTER SIX

SARAH'S skin flushed pink with shame as she felt the cutting edge of Daniel's words. She might have known that he'd take pleasure in pointing out just how deeply she'd let herself down—let Philip down. She must have been mad to let it happen. That was what it was: a kind of madness; a few moments of complete and utter insanity. The guilt would stay with her for ever.

She tidied herself up, averting her face from him as she did so, and took refuge in clearing away the remains of the picnic, putting the things they had used back into the hamper. Without a word, Daniel picked it up and carried it to the car.

The journey back was uncomfortable, almost silent. When he spoke to her, Sarah answered him in clipped tones—not wanting to talk to him, just wishing that she could be as far away from him as it was possible to be. If she could have managed it she would have gone back to Wellbrook on the train but he would hear none of that.

'I'll see you home, and that's an end to it.'

An end. It had been a weekend of firsts and now it was over, and maybe he would be going out of her life. She wished that she could forget that he had ever been part of it.

She was glad that she had arrived home before

Philip returned from his trip to the coast. It gave her time to shower away the memory of the afternoon, letting the cool spray of the water wash the heat from her skin.

She looked at herself in the mirror in the bathroom—wondering why it was that the warm caress of Daniel's hands stayed with her, why she could still feel his stroking fingers as though he was in the room with her now.

Sarah closed her mind firmly on such thoughts, concentrating instead on dressing carefully and rearranging the pleat in her hair. When Philip knocked on the door of the cottage some time later she dabbed a little perfume on her wrists and temples then hurried downstairs to greet him.

'Mmm, you smell delicious,' he murmured, hugging her close. 'How was your day? You went on a vintage car run, didn't you? I expect it was different, at any rate. Pity we didn't think to organise something on those lines for our Open Day—transport displays are a good money-spinner. Did you know we did tremendously well yesterday? My father was really pleased by the amount we collected. He's been in a good mood all day.'

'I'm glad,' she said, taking him into the sitting room. 'Does that mean everything went well for you? Did you make an offer for the machinery?'

Philip sat down next to her on the plump-cushioned settee. 'It went well enough, I suppose. We had a look at what was on offer but it wasn't really what we wanted, after all.

'For some time now I've been talking to my father

about expanding the business and he's beginning to come around to my way of thinking. The thing is that to have any kind of success we need to go for more modern, up-to-date equipment. We must move with the times if we're to stay on top.'

'So, is he going to go for that?'

Philip was enthusiastic about his work and, right now, Sarah was glad that he was full of talk about it because it meant that he wasn't pressing her for news of her day. She would sooner put that far behind her.

He was very proud of the family business and he was ambitious enough to want to make changes; to branch into areas they hadn't tried before. Sarah listened to him now and tried to share his excitement. He had a lot of plans and she wanted to be as supportive as she could.

They went out for the evening and had a pleasant enough time but later on Sarah could feel the beginnings of a headache and Philip, concerned and thoughtful as ever, brought her home so that she could have an early night.

Things soon went back to normal once the holiday period was over. Margaret returned to school, and Sarah went to help her father with the shop. They weren't very busy but her father went through the stock, rearranging things, while Sarah saw to the occasional customer and dealt with any repairs that came along.

Often, over the next few weeks, Sarah found her thoughts straying. She wondered where Daniel was now; whether he was still back at Houghton Wood or whether he was filming again. What was he thinking now? What was he doing? Her mind was filled with images of him—the sunlight dancing over the dark silk of his hair, the fleeting amusement in his keen, intelligent eyes.

Then she would shake herself mentally and try to throw off the pictures that had lodged in her head. They had no business being there. She must not think about him.

One evening Margaret switched on the television, tuning in to a talk show, and said brightly, 'Isn't that our man, Daniel? It is. Doesn't he look well? He's just back from South America from the sound of things.'

Sarah's gaze was fixed on the screen. She felt strangely breathless, her lungs suddenly tight and her heart thumping in an erratic, jerky fashion against the wall of her chest. She didn't want to watch; it oughtn't to exert such a pull on her but she couldn't turn her eyes away.

She wished that Aunt Margaret wouldn't chatter on so much so that Sarah would be able to hear what was being said. She might miss something and she badly wanted to know what he had been doing these past weeks; what his plans were.

Daniel looked directly at the camera just then and it felt as though he was looking straight at her. But of course he wasn't—it was just a lens, a piece of technical equipment, and he'd look where the cameraman indicated. He was used to being filmed.

A shiver ran from the nape of her neck down her spine and through her limbs. For a moment she felt empty, alone, utterly desolate, but there was no reason for her to feel that way, was there? She had Philip and they were getting engaged in just a few weeks; their future was mapped out for them and it was going to be absolutely fine.

There was no reason on earth why her head should be constantly filled with thoughts of Daniel. He was like a virus that she couldn't shake off. He left her feverish and out of sorts and she had a terrible feeling that there was no cure for what ailed her.

The programme came to an end, and she took herself off to bed. Apparently he was working on another book; a study of large cats this time — pumas, cheetahs, lions and tigers, all the cat family and their habitats. There would be colour photographs and sketches and it would be angled towards the children's end of the book market. It would probably sell well to schools and Margaret was pleased about that.

Sarah undressed for bed and sat at her dressing table, brushing her hair. Daniel would be at the Hall, then, putting the book together. Just a two-hour drive away but it seemed like a thousand miles of wasteland between there and here. Biting her lip, she absently put down the brush and heard it catch against the side of a photo frame, sending it skidding on to the floor.

There was a small crash, the sound of glass cracking, and she looked down in dismay to see Philip's face through the broken glass still smiling up at her.

Tears sprang to her eyes. 'Oh, Philip,' she whispered. 'I'm sorry. I'm so sorry. I don't know what's the matter with me. I feel so odd these days. But I'll make it up to you, really I will. I won't give you cause to doubt me.'

The next few days were hotter than ever. It was late June and Margaret was busy at school with various outings. She liked this time of year. Visits could be arranged without bad weather being too much of a worry and there were always treats for the children while the teachers made preparations for the end of term.

Sarah was glad to be out of the hot sun, working in the shop where it was cool most of the time. She had been on her own for most of the afternoon because her father had driven into town to see the property agent. She didn't mind that. She was tired, though, as she locked up and headed back to the cottage. The last few nights she hadn't slept well and maybe she'd have a tepid shower and listen to some quiet music after her evening meal.

She walked around the back of the house and let herself into the kitchen. Aunt Margaret must be in the sitting room because she could hear her talking to someone, cheerful laughter in her voice. Perhaps she'd brought a colleague home with her from school. Sarah put her bag down on the pine table and went to see.

'Hello, Sarah.' Daniel's deep voice wrapped itself around her consciousness, stunning her as she walked into the room.

She stood very still, taking in a sudden, quick breath, before she recovered enough to answer him in his own casual tone.

'Daniel. What a surprise to see you here again.'

'Is it? I managed to find a free day in my schedule and phoned Margaret a day or so ago to see if she wanted me to visit her school.'

'Of course I said yes straight away,' Margaret chimed in, 'and told him to hotfoot it down here as soon as ever he could make it. The children loved him but, then, I knew they would. He told them such stories! They were mesmerised.'

'I'd no idea,' Sarah said. 'You didn't mention he was coming.'

'Didn't I, dear?' Margaret began to search for her big leather bag. 'Well, so much has been happening just lately. There's been such a lot to arrange.'

It wasn't like Margaret to forget to mention anything and Sarah looked at her suspiciously for a second or two. There was nothing untoward in her expression, though; just a blithe innocence and Sarah had to be satisfied with that answer. If she'd known that Daniel was going to come here she'd have made certain she was somewhere else.

'I must be off,' Margaret said now. 'It's parents' evening and my first appointment is in half an hour. You will look after Daniel for me, won't you, Sarah? I promised him tea and scones but we were so busy talking...'

Sarah watched Margaret leave the room and turned back slowly to face Daniel, who had risen to his feet. He was every bit as lithe and muscular as she had remembered—his clothes expertly cut, the trousers moulding his strong legs and his cool-looking shirt drawing her attention to the broad sweep of his shoulders and the lean, flat wall of his stomach.

'I heard you'd been in South America,' she said. 'It seems to have deepened your tan. It suits you.'

'Thanks. I could say the same about you. You're looking beautiful as ever. A bit tired, perhaps. Have you been working too hard? Or is Philip keeping you up at night?'

'That's none of your business,' she retorted sharply, and he laughed but there was no humour in it and his eyes were darkly cynical.

'I bought you a present,' he said, waving a hand towards the coffee-table. 'And, before you think of refusing, they're signed copies so they'll be no more use to me.'

She saw two of his books lying there and she said quickly, 'I wouldn't dream of refusing, though I was thinking of treating myself on my birthday. I didn't think you'd remember.'

'You mean you hoped I'd forget.' Daniel smiled faintly, his glance moving slowly over her. 'That wasn't a likely prospect. I've an excellent memory.'

Sarah knew that he wasn't talking about the books any longer and that made her hot to the roots of her hair. 'I'll put them with our collection,' she muttered, glad of the chance to turn away. All their very special books were kept on a shelf made for the purpose and she placed them carefully, knowing that she would read them as soon as he'd gone.

'How are things going at the shop?' he asked. 'Have you found a buyer?'

'Not yet. Philip thinks things will pick up now that we're into the summer.'

'It's possible. Did he get the machinery he went after?'

'No. He thinks they should go after something more up to date. They're thinking of expansion.'

'So they should if they're to compete in the market-place. They should be looking at computerised equipment; learning new techniques.'

'You should have been a businessman yourself,' she murmured. 'You seem to know a lot about the commercial world.'

He shrugged. 'I should do. I helped my father manage the estate for as long as I can remember. The farm has always brought in a good income but you need your wits about you to see that it continues that way.'

Sarah felt a stab of interest. 'Does that mean you don't need to do the television work or write the books?'

'Those are things I enjoy doing.'

'You're very fortunate,' she said, the corners of her mouth lifting. 'How many of us can say we love our work and do it for sheer joy?'

'Does Philip enjoy his work?'

'He's keen to do well. I've always respected his ambition.'

Daniel's blue eyes regarded her steadily. 'Does he know what happened between us?'

She hadn't been expecting that question. It caught her off guard, slipping stealthily in like a watchful cat on the prowl. Her throat was uncomfortably dry all of a sudden and she swallowed carefully, composing her features into what she hoped was cool disregard. It wouldn't do to give Daniel an edge.

'What happened?' she repeated. 'Nothing happened.'

'So you didn't tell him.' He looked at her thoughtfully, his gaze penetrating. 'That's interesting.'

'I can't think why,' she said, striving for an offhand note. 'It wasn't important; it meant nothing. It was just a mistake that came about because I was hot and tired and not thinking straight. I'd had too much to drink. If I'd had all my wits about me you wouldn't have got within a yard of me, so why should I tell him?'

'That's a whole catalogue of reasons,' he said, his voice silky smooth, 'all to explain how nothing happened. You weren't affected in any way? You didn't feel anything when I kissed you?'

'Of course I wasn't affected. Oh, the sun might have clouded my judgement a little, made me hazy for a while, along with the wine. But you can't seriously think there was anything more to it than that. In fact, I lost track of who I was with. I thought for a while it was Philip who was kissing me.' Her throat closed on the lie; then she added huskily, 'It was a bit of a shock to discover that it was you the whole time.'

'You thought I was Philip?' Daniel was angry now. She could feel the rumble of it beneath the surface and could see the hard muscle in his jaw beginning to flex.

Perhaps it had been a mistake to throw in that last

bit, she thought wildly. She had forgotten that when she had first met him he had brought to mind one of those large jungle cats he knew so much about. Or perhaps he had lulled her into a false sense of security because, right now, he appeared to be every bit as savagely, dangerously, feral as a panther about to pounce.

'It was just a kiss,' Sarah muttered. 'Nothing to get excited about.'

'Of course not,' he agreed in a voice that was frighteningly soft. 'And you would never get excited about Philip's kisses, would you? But I do think I should make sure that from now on you'll at least be able to differentiate between the two of us.'

His hand shot out to manacle her wrist and she realised, too late, that she ought to have backed away while the going was good. In his present mood, though, she doubted that she'd have got much further than a couple of strides.

He jerked her to him, his free hand pushing against the nape of her neck so that she wasn't able to resist the swift descent of his mouth on hers. He kissed her fiercely, crushing the softness of her lips with such heated, urgent demand that her protests were muffled and her heart began to throb with such a hectic rhythm that she felt the blood drumming in her ears.

She was held captive against the hard length of his body and when his arms circled her all she could feel was him; all she could think of was the way his hands were moving in delicious, sensual exploration over her spine, her waist, her hips, shaping every soft curve with growing intimacy.

She was lost in a bewildering riot of sensation, a breathy little groan escaping her as his mouth shifted and she registered the hot glide of his tongue over the vulnerable arch of her throat, dipping to trace the long V of her blouse.

Daniel's hand possessively claimed the rounded swell of her breast, weighing its soft fullness in his palm while his thumb lightly teased the firming nub into tingling response. A betraying sigh shuddered on her lips and she knew that she ought to be pushing him away but that she would not. She was locked into a spiral of need and there was no going back.

Sarah felt his smile against her skin, heard the satisfaction in his voice as he muttered thickly, 'You're not going to forget me so readily now, are you, Sarah? My sweet, *lying* Sarah. You're as hungry as I am for this. Deny it if you can.'

Deftly he drew her into the muscled strength of his thighs. She sensed the heat being generated in him; knew the power of his masculine need and a shock wave of answering desire rippled through her entire body. She gasped against his throat with the sheer ecstasy of feeling, her breathing ragged and out of control.

Her fingers curled into his hair as pleasure pooled inside her, drowning out all coherent thought, but just as she would have clung to him more she felt the firm grasp of his hands around her arms, pushing her from him.

She was bemused by his actions, staring at him dark-eyed and wary, because one moment she'd been on fire and the next he was dowsing the flames by coldly distancing himself from her.

'Daniel, I—'

'I heard someone,' he said drily. 'In the kitchen. Your father, maybe? You might like a minute or two to get yourself together—unless, of course, it takes less time than that for you to convince yourself nothing happened.'

She steeled herself not to flinch at the mockery in his tone. For a short while she had forgotten how much she had needed to avoid him; how dangerous he was to her feeling of well-being; and now he was telling her that the whole thing had been a simple exercise to prove his point.

He wanted her—there was no disputing that—but it was a fleeting thing; something he could switch off with no lasting after-effect whenever it became necessary. For her it was not as simple as that. She had succumbed to a momentary weakness that would have a far more profound effect on her.

What she experienced with Daniel was a purely physical thing, wasn't it? He stirred a wildness in her that she had never recognised as part of her make-up and that was a frightening thing for her to discover about herself. That she was capable of feeling such exhilaration, such a fever of emotion.

Sarah didn't think that she would ever know that same heated passion with Philip—he was a gentler, much more reserved man and she had always liked that about him. It had never occurred to her to want more.

They were to share their lives together and surely other things were more important? Things like shared interests, common goals, the love of family and the company of mutual friends. She must not let her thoughts of Daniel intrude and tear apart the fabric of her life.

He was no friend of her family, not when you looked carefully at how he had stepped into her world. He might get on well with Margaret but what had he ever done for her father except bring him pain and distress?

Her gaze went to the door as it opened on her father. She carefully avoided looking at Daniel.

'There you are,' William said. 'And Daniel, too. Margaret said you'd be dropping in.' He smiled at them both but it was a weary smile that faded a little as he looked at Daniel. His skin had a greyish tinge to it and Sarah was worried by that. 'Did everything go well at the shop after I left?' he wanted to know, glancing at her as he took off his thin jacket.

It was a question he often asked and, since there was no day when they had hordes of customers clamouring to make their purchases, Sarah's answer was usually the same.

'Just fine.'

'Good.' To Daniel, he said soberly, 'I've been meaning to phone you. I expect you want to speak to me while you're here. Perhaps we should go through to the study and talk?'

Daniel nodded agreement, his blue eyes narrowing

on the older man and then shifting to move coolly over Sarah as she started to walk to the door.

She said shortly, 'Aunt Margaret left something for the microwave, Dad. Don't forget to eat it, will you? I have to go out. I'm to meet Philip in a few minutes.'

Daniel's gaze splintered to a glittering point of light, following her movements as she left the room. She held her head high but she felt the sting of that glance on the back of her neck long after she had closed the door behind her.

CHAPTER SEVEN

WHEN Sarah returned home after spending the evening with Philip, Daniel had gone from the house and she was glad of that. It had been difficult enough getting through each day with her thoughts persistently revolving around Daniel but to have him close at hand, provoking, demanding, making her face everything she was trying to forget, was somehow much worse.

At breakfast next day she swallowed hot coffee and watched her father going carefully through his post. He wasn't saying much but his expression was grim and she guessed that things must be bad. Just how bad were they, though? It worried her that Daniel had visited with her father yesterday but it worried her even more that, face to face, both men had seemed in serious mood.

Margaret had left for school half an hour earlier to see a couple of classes off on a trip and Sarah was thankful for that because it gave her the chance to be alone in the house with her father. She knew that he didn't like to talk about his problems in front of Margaret and this seemed as good an opportunity as any to try to get him to air them.

'More bills?' she queried now, and he nodded, pushing a handful of brown envelopes to one side. 'Will we be able to pay them?'

He sighed heavily. 'Not all of them but I'll sort through to find the most urgent ones. I'll spend some time on them this evening when I get back from the shop.'

'I suppose paying off the loan is making things really tough. Did Daniel talk to you about that yesterday? Was there a problem?'

'It's been difficult,' he admitted. He looked away, almost as though he couldn't face her, then he said gruffly, 'I've been finding it hard to get the money together and I missed a payment. I needed to angle for more time.'

'Oh, Dad—' Sarah was horror-struck. 'Why didn't you say anything about what was happening? I wish you wouldn't keep things to yourself so much. We could have talked this through; worked something out together. The last thing we need is for Daniel to have an excuse to put pressure on us. We could be bankrupted.'

'I know, I know. I keep thinking that when the shop is sold I can pay off a lump sum and then things might ease up.' He split open another envelope and took out the contents but he wasn't looking at the papers in his hands. His grey eyes were distant. 'The trouble is that the few offers we're getting are far too low.'

'And in the meantime we're struggling to keep our heads above water.' She frowned, then said, 'I told you I want to do whatever I can. I'll find another job and then I'll be able to help more financially. Have you talked to Aunt Margaret about the way things are? I'm sure she'd want to help, too.'

'No. No, you mustn't do that.' He sent her a fierce, determined look. 'Time enough for you to start searching for another job when the shop's sold. I need you there now because at the moment the mainstay of our work is repairs and, anyway, I can't always be there.

'As to Margaret, she isn't to know any of this. She thinks I'm selling up because I feel it's time to retire and I want her to go on thinking that. I'm only telling you any of this because it affects you personally. We'll keep Margaret out of it.'

It was pride, she supposed. Margaret was successful, a professional, and he must feel that he was letting the side down. It wasn't his fault that things had gone so badly wrong but Sarah had long since stopped trying to press that point home.

'We'll sort something out,' she said. 'I'll put an advert in the paper to say I'm providing a book-repair service. That will widen my territory a bit and it should bring in a little more income.'

Philip called in at the shop later in the week. He looked harassed, she thought, yet at the same time there was a kind of suppressed excitement about him.

'I couldn't wait until this evening to tell you, Sarah. I've just heard the news and I'm up to my eyes in arrangements. It's all happening so quickly that I scarcely know where to start.'

'Try the beginning,' she laughed. 'Calm down and tell me what's happened.'

He leaned against the grandfather clock, his hands hooked loosely into his trouser pockets. 'I should have told you what my father had in mind before this but I wasn't sure it would come to anything.'

'Then tell me now,' she said. 'I'm intrigued.'

He gave her a quick smile. 'You know we were thinking of updating our methods, thinking of new systems and so on? Well, there's an opportunity for me to go to Europe on a visit—spend some time with a company over there, live with the owner's family and generally learn more about their techniques across the board; management, production and so on.

'They also have a complex out in the Far East and I can move on to look at that after a few weeks.'

'That sounds like a chance in a million,' she said.

'It is. It will be a real boost for our business if we can develop new processes. Of course we'll be working with the company on agreements for opening up new outlets over here.'

'But how did it all come about? Does Maurice know these people? Are they friends of his?'

'He'd heard of them, of course, but it was Courtenay who suggested the arrangement. Apparently my father had spent some time talking to him about one thing and another and Courtenay mentioned that he has connections over there. After that it was just a question of settling details with the owners.'

'Daniel made this possible?' She couldn't stop the sudden prickling sensation that ran over her skin. 'He's behind all these arrangements?'

'That's right. He dealt with all the negotiations

from the beginning so that everything went through as smooth as butter.'

Sarah felt a little sick as her stomach muscles twisted into a tense knot. What was going on? Daniel must be doing this for a reason and she couldn't help but feel threatened by the situation. He wasn't doing this out of the kindness of his heart, aiming to help the Prescott-Searles. He was planning something and she wished that she knew what it was.

'Darling?' Philip must have noticed her abstraction because he was looking at her now with a faintly anxious expression. 'You don't mind, do you? I know it will mean my being away for a few weeks but we'll be able to talk on the phone. It isn't as though we won't be able to keep in touch.'

'Of course I don't mind,' she hastened to reassure him. 'I'm very happy for you, really I am. Do you think you'll be able to get home for the occasional weekend? Or maybe I could come over to see you.'

'We'll have to see how it goes. It might be difficult at first because I know there will be a few conferences going on at the weekends and I really need to be there. Perhaps it won't be too bad for us—I expect you'll be so busy organising the sale of the shop that the weeks will seem to race by and you'll hardly know I've been away.'

Sarah didn't share his optimism about the shop but she wasn't going to cast a blight on his happiness by saying so. 'How long is there before you have to go away?' she asked.

'A couple of days.'

'In that case,' she said in a decisive tone, 'we had better make the most of the time we have left.'

She wasn't particularly worried about him going away. Of course she would miss him. Their routine of spending time together in the evenings and at weekends when they weren't working would be completely disrupted but she would look for other things to fill that gap.

She would be able to see more of her friends; she would catch up on her reading, listen to music or get out her sewing machine and run up a few cool cotton things for the summer. He was probably right when he said that the weeks would race by...and that bothered her a little. Oughtn't she to feel something more, some sense of loss or deprivation?

But theirs was a comfortable, easy relationship. It ran smoothly with no major ups and downs, no great swings of emotion, and perhaps that was why she wasn't concerned in that respect. Philip would be back with her soon enough and they would go on as before.

What really worried her was Daniel's part in all this. What was he trying to do? Was he trying to keep them apart? Did he mean to make himself such a part of her existence that she couldn't live without him?

Sarah couldn't let him do that. She had to get him out of her system once and for all because she knew, deep down, that he had the power to destroy her. He made her feel things that she had never thought were possible; had brought to life in her sensations and emotions that she hadn't thought herself capable of experiencing. He made her feel too much, that was the trouble, and it frightened her and left her feeling churned up inside.

Over the next few days she had other things to occupy her mind as she became increasingly anxious about her father's health. He never looked strong at the best of times and just lately he wasn't breathing so well and Sarah suspected that he was in a certain amount of pain.

She wanted to call a doctor but he stopped her, saying, 'I'll be fine. I'll take a tablet and then I'll be myself again. You go off to the shop and I'll stay home and work on the accounts. No sense in paying accountant's fees when I can just as easily do the job myself. I can sit here quietly at the table and get on with it without any distractions.'

'You're a stubborn old thing,' Sarah told him with a faint smile and a smattering of exasperation. 'Sometimes I think that dealing with you is like banging my head against a brick wall.' She stood over him, though, while he swallowed a tablet and in a while some of his colour did begin to return. 'Just promise me that if you feel any worse you'll ring me at the shop. I'll come straight home.'

'I promise.'

It was half-day closing so she would be going home anyway at lunchtime after she had done the weekly shop. Her father didn't call so she went to the supermarket, picking out the best buys and trying to think what she would do for the evening meal.

When she arrived back at the cottage he looked

strained and ill and, since he still wouldn't hear of her getting the doctor, she insisted that he went up to bed. She plumped up his pillows and saw him settled, vowing that like it or not she'd call the surgery if he didn't show any signs of improvement.

When she looked in on him an hour later, after she had put away the groceries and tidied the kitchen, he was sleeping peacefully and it was clear that the rest was doing him some good. She crept out of his room, closing the door behind her, and went downstairs.

Sarah had brought some work home with her from the shop—another book that needed attention to the cover, velvet this time which was easier to handle and shouldn't take her too long.

It was satisfying work, making something look as good as new and seeing the pleasure light up a customer's face when they saw the end result. For half an hour or so she was engrossed in what she was doing and when the doorbell rang it seemed like an intrusion, jarring her concentration.

She went to answer it, ready to hear the patter of a door-to-door salesman but it was Daniel she saw standing there and she stared at him, wide-eyed, her stomach doing a curious little flip-over.

'Aren't you going to invite me in?' he drawled, jerking her out of her dazed preoccupation so that she stepped back and silently held the door open for him to come through.

'What do you want, Daniel?' she asked belatedly, when he had walked through to the cosy kitchen. 'Why are you here?'

'I promised Margaret I'd let her have some slides for school.' He put a package down on the worktop and it said something about how fazed she was to see him because she hadn't even noticed that he had been carrying one.

'She won't be back until late,' Sarah said. 'She has a staff meeting after school.'

'I'll leave them here for her.' He looked around the kitchen—at her work on the table, at the neatness of the room. 'I remembered it was your half-day at the shop. Is your father about? I noticed his car was outside.'

Sarah's protective instincts came surging to the fore. 'You can't see him,' she said. 'He isn't seeing anyone.'

His dark brows lifted at that. 'Are you telling me that I can't even say hello?'

'He's not well,' she persisted, 'and right now he's sleeping. His heart isn't strong; he's been under a strain these last few weeks and you're not to disturb him.'

'Am I being warned off?'

'If that's how you want to see it.'

He considered her for a moment, his eyes narrowed and speculative. 'So what's causing all this strain? Is it the shop?'

Sarah ought to have known that he wouldn't leave it at that. She didn't want to have to answer but she said, 'The property market's been slow for a long time now. It's frustrating, I suppose, having things drag on.'

'So things are getting worse?' He seemed to be

musing aloud and went on, 'His financial situation must be going into a decline.'

She was beginning to wish that she hadn't said anything but she didn't want him going away with the wrong idea.

'You don't have to worry about the money he owes you,' she said shortly, trying to put some conviction into the words. 'I'm sure there'll be no problem there. In any case, you can talk things through with me while my father's ill. I shall be taking care of his business dealings until such time as he can see to them himself. He's left everything in my hands.'

She was lying through her teeth but she said it as steadily as she could manage and excused herself with the knowledge that she was only doing it to keep her father from further worry. There must be some solution to his anxieties.

'Has he?' Daniel's stare was watchful.

'He has. I know there has been a bit of a hiccup just lately and he hasn't made the payment he should have but it's only because he's been under the weather and he's let things slide. I could write you a cheque now.'

She reached for her bag and pulled out her cheque-book, hoping that whatever her father owed didn't come to more than she had in her account.

'I don't think so,' Daniel said. 'I'll wait for your father to deal with it...when he's able.'

'There's no need for that. I'd like to get things cleared up so that when he's well again he'll have no backlog of problems. You'll have to just remind me of the exact amount that's due.'

He studied her for a moment without saying anything and when she looked at the taut, hard line of his mouth she gained the strong impression that he was battling silently to suppress his anger.

'Do you seriously imagine,' he said with a rasp, 'that I would be concerned over a few missed payments?'

A few. Not one payment but several. Sarah felt a swift pang of anxiety but she tried not to let him see that the news had shaken her. 'My father is,' she told him. 'Or, at least, something's putting him on edge.'

'His edginess,' Daniel said abrasively, 'probably has more to do with the sum total of his debt than with anything else.'

Sarah's fingers closed on the soft leather of her bag. 'There we have it, then. Once the shop is sold his worries will be over and he'll pay off what he owes in a lump sum. Then there'll be no need for monthly payments and we can forget the whole matter.'

He gave her a dry smile. 'You know, Sarah, you really don't make a very good liar. You should never have tried to make me believe that your father put you in the picture and gave you the go-ahead to step in for him.'

It was her turn to raise her brows. She did it casually, as though she thought he was slightly off balance. 'I don't know what you think you mean. My father explained the situation to me—'

'But not the full facts, apparently. How much do

you expect the shop will fetch, supposing you get a buyer?'

She named the highest price she could think of, adding a few hundred on top, and was startled to see him shake his head.

'Even if you were lucky enough to get that, it wouldn't cover the debt.'

A chill crept through her veins. 'You're talking the full amount, including interest,' she said, her voice a little shaky. 'Of course we've made provision for that.'

'I'm not including interest,' Daniel said. 'Your father borrowed a large amount several years ago which included the purchase price of this cottage. Then the recession started to bite and he borrowed more.'

'I know that,' she said. 'He told me. But years ago the shop and cottage would have been bought at a much lower price than they'll fetch now.'

'I'm afraid that isn't true. The market value of the property has fallen over these last years and he won't be able to cover anywhere near the amount he owes.'

'You're saying that the house is at risk as well?' It was what she had feared all along but she had kept on hoping that it wouldn't come to it. She was icy cold, shock sending tremors to pulse through her limbs, leaving her weak and her legs with no substance to them. Blindly she felt for a chair and sat down.

It was no wonder that her father was in such a stressed state. The only surprising thing was that he'd managed to hide the severity of the situation from her for so long. From Margaret, too. Why was he so secretive? And why on earth would Daniel's mother make her father a loan of such magnitude? None of it made sense. And none of these questions helped her to find a way that she could begin to deal with the situation.

'There must be some way out of this,' Sarah said hoarsely. 'You could give us more time—'

'What good will that do? He's already had years.'

Her lips were dry as dust and she moistened them lightly with the tip of her tongue. 'I have some savings... I could get a loan from the bank and pay you myself.' Her hands twisted wretchedly in her lap. 'There must be some way I can help my father... I'd do anything to help him, Daniel, anything.' She lifted her gaze to him, distress adding the bright sheen of banked tears to her eyes.

'Perhaps you do have a price after all,' Daniel said thoughtfully and she flinched at the cynicism in his tone.

'What do you mean?'

'I think you know what I mean, well enough. It isn't money I want from you, Sarah.' She tried to shake her head but he went on in a low, roughened tone, 'I want you. I've wanted you from the moment I set eyes on you and what I feel hasn't abated a fraction since then. Instead it's become steadily worse—like a fire that's burning out of control, raging inside me. I want you and it's changed my life; changed the kind of person I am. I don't even much care what I have to do to get you.'

'No,' she whispered. 'No. You can't say these

things to me. It's impossible. I'm not free—I've never been free—I'm getting engaged...on my birthday... I love Philip.'

'You don't love him.' She had never seen him so grimly implacable. 'A woman in love doesn't respond to another man the way you respond to me. The only reason you won't tell him about us is because then you'll have to admit what it is that you're really feeling. Stop lying to yourself, Sarah. Face up to it.'

'I can't—I won't. You can't make me. I wish you'd go away and stay away and leave me in peace.'

'That isn't going to happen. You know it isn't. I think you realised that from the first. You're responsible for this fire that's burning me up; you're the only one who can tame it and I won't let you run away from me and pretend it never happened.'

A touch of bitter anger laced Daniel's voice and as Sarah looked up into the flickering, leaping flame of his eyes she recognised what it was that set him apart from other men. Inside him was a rock-hard core of determination that meant that once he had made up his mind on something he would pursue it to the very end. No matter what the cost. He would let nothing get in his way.

'I don't believe any of this,' she protested huskily. 'None of this is happening. It isn't real; it's just a dream.'

'It isn't a dream,' he said softly. 'It's very real... and the only question is what are we going to do about it?'

CHAPTER EIGHT

'WE AREN'T going to do anything about it,' Sarah countered shakily. 'You aren't part of my life. I'm not going to let you be part of it. Philip means everything to me. We've been together for such a long time—I can't let you tear us apart.'

'If you felt strongly enough about him I wouldn't be able to,' Daniel said with callous disregard for her feelings. 'You're clinging to the fact that you've been together for so long because he's like an old shoe, comfortable and familiar; you feel safe with him and you're not quite sure how you'd feel without him. Well, now he's away and you're going to get the chance to find out.'

Her fingers twisted against the wooden frame of her chair. 'I knew you were up to something,' she said, her tone suddenly aggrieved. 'You've been planning something all along.'

His blue glance mocked her. 'You were well aware of what's been happening between us. Even you couldn't ignore the sparks that fly about whenever we get within touching distance of each other. You surely didn't expect me to let things drift?'

She ran a faintly trembling hand through her hair, the coolness of her fingertips going a little way to ease the throbbing at her temples.

'What is it you want, Daniel?'

141

His mouth twisted in a crooked smile. 'You said you wanted to help your father. I'm willing to give you that opportunity.'

'How?' She looked at him uncertainly, a pulse flickering unevenly at the base of her throat.

'I want you to come and stay at the Hall for a while. Do some work for me.'

Her eyes widened. 'What kind of work?'

'Bookbinding...repairs. There are several manuscripts that need gathering into book form, some very old and precious books that need care and attention.' He looked at the equipment spread out on the kitchen table, at the rectangle of velvet and the tools for marking out the title on the front cover and spine. 'I've seen the work you do and I know you would do a good job. What do you say?'

'I could do that here,' Sarah said carefully. 'I would have done it for you before this if you'd asked.'

An amused glint came into his eyes. 'But I want you to stay at the Hall,' he murmured softly. 'That's the one condition I'm imposing.'

Her breath caught in a shuddery spasm in her chest. That one condition could prove to be her undoing and that was exactly what he was banking on. Daniel didn't think that her love for Philip would stand the test...and she couldn't push away the shaky feeling that he might well be right. She hadn't done so very well up to now. Daniel was exerting a pull on her that she was finding harder and harder to resist.

'And in return?'

'In return I'll give William as much time as he needs and I'll write off a quarter of the debt. Is it a deal?'

She swallowed hard against the sudden tightness in her throat. As deals went it was more than generous. One that he knew she couldn't afford to turn down. It was only the underlying cost that worried her; the knowledge that while her mind was telling her to exercise caution her inner self was beginning to glow at the prospect of spending time with him—days and nights when there would be just the two of them.

Perhaps she didn't know what was right and what was wrong any more. Philip was away and her heart was thumping against her ribs just at the thought of being with this man and that had to be bad, didn't it? She must not let him weave his spell around her; she must not hurt Philip—he didn't deserve to be treated that way.

'My father would want to know why you were doing that,' she pointed out anxiously. 'He has his pride.'

Daniel shrugged. 'When the next payment becomes due I'll make up some story about investing the income and working out a new deal. It shouldn't be too difficult to convince him.'

'I'm only agreeing to come over to the house to work,' she said, a trace of doubt in her voice. 'I'm not committing myself to anything else.'

His gaze rested on her, dark and unfathomable. 'That's enough to be going on with.'

Sarah wasn't sure that she was entirely happy with

that answer but he wasn't forcing her into anything and her father stood to gain both his self-respect and his health.

'I'd need to wait until he's feeling better,' she said cautiously. 'I couldn't leave him while he's ill. Besides, there would be no one to look after the shop.'

'That's fair enough.' He smiled into her eyes. 'Will you call me and let me know how he's doing?'

'Yes, of course.'

'Good.' He glanced down at the slim gold watch on his wrist and grimaced. 'I have to go. My sister and her brood are coming over for a visit this evening.'

'I'll see you to the door.'

At the front door he said, 'Give my regards to your father. Tell him I hope he'll soon be feeling much better.'

'I will.'

It was a couple of weeks before her father was well enough to return to work. She'd called the doctor in spite of his protests and it was a relief to know that it had only been a mild chest infection which had aggravated his underlying condition. He had to rest for a while but after that he could go back to the shop and, provided he took things easy, there should be no lasting after-effects.

He was pleased when she told him that she was to spend some time at the Hall, working on Daniel's books.

'It will bring in some extra cash,' she told him,

'and that will help out, won't it?' Daniel wasn't paying her but she wasn't telling her father that. She would slip some money unobtrusively into the shop's account from her own and her father would be none the wiser.

Philip phoned the evening before she was to leave for Houghton Wood.

'Why do you have to stay there?' he wanted to know. 'Couldn't you do the work from home?'

'It would have been convenient, wouldn't it?' she agreed. She wasn't going to tell him what she'd learned about her father's debt. It was her father's business and no one else's. Besides, Philip had never shown much interest whenever she'd mentioned the shop. He tended to discount it since it didn't figure in his grand scheme of things.

'I expect Daniel doesn't want things taken away from the Hall,' she said. 'A lot of the books he has in the library are very valuable. Perhaps they're only insured while they're on the premises.'

'I don't like the idea of you being there with him,' Philip complained. 'He's footloose and fancy-free and I wouldn't put it past him to try something on with you. It runs in the blood, you know. The Courtenays have a reputation for that kind of thing.'

Sarah laughed at that. 'Whatever do you mean? Was there a French count or someone in their murky past who had his wicked way with one of the maidservants?'

'It's a bit nearer home than that.' Philip didn't take kindly to her amusement—she could tell that from his tone. 'Haven't you heard about the scandal in that family? It was hushed up for years but since his grandfather died people have been talking about it more openly. His grandfather was supposed to have had a thing going with the seamstress just a few years after he married. There was a child but I imagine he never acknowledged it because of his wife.'

'He can't just have ignored his own child, surely?' Sarah protested. Though when she thought back to that portrait of Daniel's grandmother and remembered what he had jokingly said about her being able to freeze him on the spot she wasn't so convinced. 'What happened to the seamstress?'

'She left the Hall before the baby was born. I think she died in childbirth. That's how the story goes, anyway.'

'So where is the child now?' she asked, feeling a pang of anguish for the mother and her baby.

'No idea,' Philip said, annoyingly.

Sarah hated stories that were unfinished. It was like watching a film on video and finding that the end had been cut off.

'I almost wish you hadn't told me any of that,' she muttered crossly. 'Anyway, all that was years ago and I'm sure I shall be quite safe up at the Hall. I shall think about you looking over your computerised machines and soaking up the atmosphere of the Far East.'

'It won't be for much longer, darling. I should be home in a couple of weeks. We'll get engaged then and we'll start making real plans for our future. I know the shop's a problem for you and I haven't been much help up to now. I've been so taken up with my own concerns that I haven't really been listening to yours. But I've had a word with my parents about it and they thought they might look into buying the place.

'Your father could stay on as manager and it would be a little part-time interest for you after we're married. Of course, they'll need to inspect the accounts to see what kind of turnover they might get but that shouldn't be too much of a problem. I'll let you know what happens.'

Sarah put down the phone in a thoughtful mood some minutes later. She wasn't sure quite how her father would react to being a manager in the shop that had been his for years but it had become part of his life and he had been very reluctant to part with it.

She didn't want to get his hopes up but she did mention to him that Philip thought that there might be a prospective buyer in the offing.

It seemed to lift his spirits, anyway, and she drove down to Houghton Wood feeling that she had at least left him in a cheerful frame of mind.

Daniel had just finished overseeing the estate's farmlands with his manager when she arrived. He walked with her into the Hall and she had trouble taking her eyes off him as he looked so fit and full of vitality. He was wearing cream-coloured trousers and a dark shirt with the cuffs rolled back so that she could see his bronzed forearms and their fine shading of dark hair.

She felt an odd urge to run her fingers over his bared skin and she had to push her hands firmly down into the pockets of her jeans out of harm's way.

He insisted that she have something to eat and drink after her journey but when she asked about the library later on he took her along there, answering her questions as they went.

Sarah had already looked into the library at the Hall on her previous visit but it had been a hurried occasion and now Daniel showed it to her properly, pointing out the various books and manuscripts that he wanted her to work on.

'There's a fifteenth-century service book which has been in the family since this place was built,' he said, 'along with the family Bible, which needs very careful handling.

'Then there are a number of household accounts which date back through the centuries—I'd like those bound into book form. They make interesting reading...there are things like itemised building costs from the earlier renovations and additions and wages bills for the various people who worked on the estate.

'Some of the housekeepers' notes, going back through the years, could be bound, too, in a separate volume or perhaps we could make a book for each housekeeper's stay. There are recipes and household hints, shopping lists, that kind of thing. Put together, they make a wonderful collection of historical data. Do you think you can do it?'

'Of course.' It was the sort of opportunity that she

had always dreamed of when she was learning to perfect her skills. To be able to look through so many manuscripts and volumes which catalogued one family's history would give her a real sense of satisfaction and making something beautiful of them appealed to her creative instincts. 'I can't wait to get started.'

'Slow down,' he said with a laugh. 'Get settled in first. Have a good look round the place.'

Sarah's room overlooked the lake. It was sumptuously furnished, with a dressing table and armchairs and even a little writing desk in one corner. There was thick carpet underfoot and velvet curtains at the windows and she had her own private bathroom adjoining, reached through a connecting door.

He'd said, 'Slow down,' but she was anxious to get started. She was here to work and she didn't want Daniel getting the idea that she'd come for any other reason. So, when she woke to glorious sunshine next day, she hurriedly washed and dressed and went down to the breakfast room, hoping that Daniel was a late riser or that he might have gone out earlier.

He was sitting at the table, however, and as she walked into the room he said, 'You're looking good this morning. Did you sleep well?'

'Very well, thanks. I woke to hear the birds singing in the tree outside my room. It was a lovely start to the day, knowing that all around me is green farmland and beautiful countryside.'

'We could spend the morning riding around the estate, if you like. I'll get the groom to saddle a couple of horses.'

It was a tempting offer and it made her hesitate for a moment but she couldn't afford to be enticed off course before she had been here five minutes.

'I don't think so,' she said. 'Thanks all the same. I'll get started on the books. Besides, I don't ride.'

'That could soon be remedied. We could fix you up with Bess—she's a thoroughly gentle mare, very placid and easy to get along with. I'd show you how to walk her. You wouldn't have any cause to be afraid.'

He was making it very difficult for her to resist. The possibility that she might be with him for just a short time, the two of them riding side by side and exploring the vast acreage of the estate, held a strong attraction for her. But she must not give in to this weakness that kept invading her will. She was not being fair to Philip.

'Perhaps...perhaps another time,' she murmured. 'I'd rather get on with what I came here for.'

'As you please,' Daniel said. 'But if you change your mind the offer's open.'

Sarah was thankful that he hadn't argued with her and over the next few days she refused more of his invitations, equally tempting.

She could have gone with him to a country inn to while away an hour or two or driven into town for an afternoon...but there was no point in thinking about what might have been. Establishing a routine was the important thing and she had managed that, working through the day and taking dinner with him in the evening. He wasn't putting pressure on her and she was glad of that.

She was used to him coming into the library each day to work on his book at a table by the window across from her. They talked a little as they worked but often there was a companionable silence between them and it was surprising how relaxed she had begun to feel when he was around. In fact, she realised with a small frown, she was beginning to miss him when he wasn't there.

At the weekend she went home to the cottage, anxious to check that her father wasn't overdoing things. On the phone he'd said that he was fine but she had to make sure. It was a long weekend. The time dragged; she was restless and distracted and her thoughts were constantly straying back to the Hall.

She wanted to see Daniel. That knowledge shocked her and made her feel desperately guilty but she couldn't deny any longer that she wanted to be with him. She was relieved when the weekend was over.

Sarah soon slipped back into the routine of working in the library each day. Daniel had greeted her on her return and it would have been so easy to let him know how she felt — by a look, a gesture — but she held back from doing that. Her feelings were raw and uncertain and she needed time to think things through.

She looked out of the window at the gardens and wondered where he was now. There was no reason why she shouldn't go and find him; see if he wanted to walk a while or just talk. But, no, she wouldn't do that. His effect on her was far too dangerous. He was like a powerful drug working its way into her system—the more she had, the more she craved.

Glancing down at the table and the equipment spread out in front of her, she had to collect her thoughts to recall what it was she had been doing. This was happening to her more and more often lately and it was disconcerting to find that her mind had strayed so completely from what she was doing.

Her gaze came to rest on the Courtenay family Bible and her mind cleared. This afternoon she was renewing the gold lettering on the cover. It was a job that needed careful attention, applying glaire to the tooled impressions to make the gold stick and then adding the gold with slow precision.

She had been bent over the work for a couple of hours or more and it was no wonder that her muscles were beginning to ache. Stretching her limbs, she arched her neck to ease the strain.

'What you need,' Daniel said, making her jump a little as he came unexpectedly into the room, 'is a massage.' He placed cool hands on her shoulders. 'Just settle back,' he ordered quietly, when she would have moved away. 'I know just the way to ease those tense muscles. You should never have worked so long without a break. You're overdoing things and that's not allowed. From now on I'm going to make sure you take a good portion of leisure time off each day.'

All the time that he was speaking his thumbs and fingers were doing delicious things to her neck and spine and, while each caress made her feel an ecstasy of delight, at the same time she felt a tiny stab of jealousy, wondering where he had learned the technique and who he had practised on.

Still, whatever he was doing was making her feel gloriously woozy—as though she'd been drinking deeply of a very fine wine.

'That feels heavenly,' Sarah murmured, a drowsy contentment creeping into her voice.

'Does it?' His head bent towards her and she registered the faint drift of his breath on her cheek and felt his warmth as he moved closer.

'Mmm. Bliss. Like floating on cotton-wool clouds as though I haven't a care in the world.'

Daniel's fingers continued to work their magic, making smooth, ever-widening circles over her neck and shoulders and down over her upper arms.

'Good. That's what I want you to feel. Without a care in the world; nothing to intrude. There's only the two of us and that's all that matters.'

The brush of his mouth was feather light on the sensitised curve between neck and shoulder, sending a melting sweetness to flow through her. He had only to touch her and a yielding weakness threatened to dissolve her limbs.

A sigh trembled on her lips. Whenever he was near her senses went into overdrive and now, as he swivelled her chair slowly around until she was facing him, she looked up into the lambent flame of his blue eyes and knew that she wanted him to kiss her properly—to take her in his arms and hold her as though nothing in the world could separate them.

He leaned towards her, his hands resting firmly on the arms of her chair, and then his mouth was seeking hers, parting her lips with an urgent passion that sparked every nerve-ending she possessed into feverish, tingling life.

She returned his kiss hungrily, her lips clinging to his, her hands lifting to restlessly stroke the muscled strength of his arms and trail in a questing path over the firm wall of his chest. The buttons of his shirt gave way beneath her roaming fingers and she encountered his smooth, firm skin with startled delight.

A groan rose huskily in her throat. She wanted more than this; she wanted to be much closer to him, her body meeting his in heated fusion.

Daniel seemed to sense what it was that she wanted and drew her towards him, his arms folding about her, the softness of her breasts crushed against him.

Neither of them registered the knocking on the door until it grew louder and then they broke suddenly away from each other, Sarah's expression becoming panicked as she tried to assemble her scattered wits.

Daniel stepped away from her, his back to the door as he quickly fastened the buttons of his shirt and straightened himself up. When the door opened he turned, looking as cool and composed as ever, while Sarah felt that she might never be the same again.

Annie came into the room, saying, 'Daniel, there's someone here to see you. Marty Franklin from the TV company. Shall I show her in?'

'Of course, Annie. I'll see her in here.'

Marty Franklin swept into the library a moment later, a tall, striking woman with shining black hair that swung in a gleaming curtain with every slight movement of her head. Her lips were full and red, her eyes a brilliant, jewelled green, her shapely body swathed in a flame-coloured dress that fitted her to perfection and would have knocked any man for six.

Sarah was prepared to hate her on sight.

'Daniel, I'm so sorry to drop in on you like this without any warning but I was in the area and I felt sure you wouldn't mind.' She looked at him through the downward sweep of her lashes and the answering quirk of Daniel's mouth told her all she needed to know.

Her glance flicked curiously to Sarah, sitting at the table, then returned to Daniel. 'I hope I'm not disturbing anything; that you're not too busy to see me?'

'Not at all, Marty,' Daniel said easily. 'Sarah is working on some of my books for me—repairing them mostly and binding one or two others.'

'Oh, really?' Marty studied Sarah more closely, her glance going swiftly over her slender figure, dismissively appraising the simple blouse and skirt that she was wearing.

'Do you work for a company that specialises in that kind of thing?' she asked Sarah.

'I work in my father's bookshop,' Sarah answered quietly. She could see that she had not impressed Marty one bit with that snippet of information.

'I hope you know what you're doing,' the other woman said coolly. 'Daniel's books are tremendously valuable. They've been in the family for generations. Some of them would be museum pieces, only he won't hear of letting them go.'

'I think Sarah knows that well enough,' Daniel remarked. 'I'm sure she'll take extra care with them. Now, what was it that you wanted to see me about?'

Marty slid her arm through his. 'I want to ask you a very special favour. I know you've been rushed off your feet this year, with one thing and another, but we want you to do another programme for us.'

'What kind of programme? I've only just come back from South America and I didn't plan on going anywhere else for a long time.'

'You're working on the book—I know. But you won't have to travel for this. We want to do a programme on you—your life, your thoughts, your home. So many people write in and want to know more about the man behind the wildlife series.' Her body moved against him in sinuous invitation. 'What do you think? Will you do it? Please say that you will.'

'I'll certainly think about it.'

'It would be such good publicity for the book,' Marty said, using a wheedling tone as she looked up into his eyes, her mouth making a provocative pout.

Daniel looked amused. 'I dare say it would.'

'Then let's talk it through,' she suggested, her voice a sultry murmur, 'somewhere more private, where I can go over all the possibilities with you.' She ignored Sarah totally, still clinging to Daniel, her fingers circling his arm possessively.

Sarah felt her stomach muscles tense, tightening

in a nauseous spasm. She wanted to look away. She didn't want to see Daniel succumbing to the clutches of this sensuous sex bomb but her gaze was fixed; while they were in the room she had to know what was happening even if it made her ill.

'All right,' Daniel said, smiling. 'We'll go and talk about it. Shall we go into the study?'

Sarah watched the pair of them walk from the room, still entwined, and she swallowed hard against the bitter gall that rose in her throat. How could he walk out with that painted mantrap? Was he really so shallow that he was ready to lap up her charms like an eager dog? But perhaps that was what men like him did. They went after the sure thing. It was casual and uncomplicated and he was a free agent. He'd always liked it that way.

She hated him for the way he'd gone off with that woman. She felt like ranting and raging at him; she wanted to pummel him with her bare hands. She hated him.

No—she subsided all at once, the breath leaving her lungs in a sudden rush. It wasn't hate she felt for Daniel. But what she did feel was so shattering that the knowledge of it hit her like a tidal wave, bursting over her in full force so that she was powerless against it. She began to tremble violently.

It wasn't hate, at all. It was love that made her feel so desperate...she loved him. It wasn't anything like what she felt for Philip. This was a searing, painful emotion that tore at her insides and made her feel utterly wretched. Seeing Daniel smiling into the eyes of another woman had made her want to claw the pair of them and that was an emotion so alien to her that it shocked her to the core. She had never felt this way about anyone before. How could she be reduced to such a wild, reckless state of mind?

She wasn't in any condition to work any longer and now she knew a frantic need to get away. It was impossible for her to stay here, knowing that the two of them were probably right this moment getting close on the buttoned leather couch in the study.

She didn't even wait to clear up the things from the desk. Instead she grabbed her purse and walked out of the house, along the curving drive and out on to the country road. She had no idea where she was going but she kept on walking until her feet ached and the muscles in her legs started to complain. Even then she kept on going.

A bus crawled to a halt by the roadside, letting off some passengers, and she climbed on to it, taking a seat by the window but seeing nothing of the countryside that passed by.

She had only herself to blame for the way she felt now. He had never made any promises and she had never been left in any doubt about his motives. He had known she wasn't free yet still he had pursued her and it must have been out of sheer devilment — the need to go after someone that he knew he couldn't have.

Sarah bit down on her lip hard, wincing as the tender flesh split. There could never be any future for her with Daniel. She wasn't the kind of woman who could settle for a light, no-strings-attached affair. How could she have been fool enough to have fallen for a man who had never shown the slightest inclination for settling down? He was quite content to roam the world, being seen alongside its most glamorous women...was with one even now.

Perhaps he'd known Marty for a long time. Maybe they had been lovers. Were still lovers. Sarah hunched over in her seat. She was feeling sick again.

When the bus reached town she wandered around for a while, then went into a cinema and sat through the film that was showing without knowing what was going on on-screen. When everyone else started to get up out of their seats and wander out, she realised that she, too, ought to make a move. She stumbled outside onto the street.

It had been late afternoon when she had left the Hall but darkness had set in now and the breeze on her skin was cool, chilling her limbs. She couldn't stay here any longer. She had to get back.

A bus took her as far as the lane and she walked the last half-mile to the house. There were lights on in some of the rooms and she wished that they were there to welcome her but knew that it could never be. She didn't belong here. Right now she didn't feel as though she belonged anywhere.

She pushed open the heavy oak door.

'Where have you been?'

Daniel's gritty voice challenged her before she had even had time to close the door behind her.

'Out,' Sarah said briefly, not wanting to talk, and went to move past him, heading for the stairs.

'Not so fast.' He moved with her, in front of her, his hand shooting out to grip the carved wooden post at the foot of the staircase. His arm blocked her way. 'You've some explaining to do.'

'Me?' Her brows shot up but she was pretending a calm she didn't feel. He looked grim and deadly angry and his powerful frame was a looming threat. He looked as though he'd like to strangle her with his bare hands. 'You're joking, of course,' she murmured. 'I don't have to explain anything to you. I just work here. Temporarily. And now I'd like to go upstairs to bed. Excuse me, please.'

'No.' His dark eyes homed in on her with savage intensity. 'I don't feel like excusing you anything. I want to know what's going on here. You just upped and disappeared. You didn't take your car; you weren't anywhere on the estate. Anything could have happened to you. Damn you, Sarah, I want an explanation.'

Sarah's shoulders lifted carelessly. 'I told you,' she said. 'I went out. I felt like getting some air. I've been cooped up in the house for such a long time and I needed to get away for a while.' She returned his gaze with one of casual indifference. 'Now, may I go to bed?'

Daniel's jaw clamped tightly. 'It's your own fault if you've been feeling cooped up. I've given you every opportunity to get out and about and relax. You chose not to.'

'But today I changed my mind. I'm sorry if you were put to any trouble trying to find me. As you can see, I'm perfectly well.' Her lashes flickered. 'You're still in my way, Daniel.'

He glowered at her but he moved to one side all

the same and she started quickly up the stairs, conscious that he was keeping pace with her.

'So, where did you go?'

'For a walk.'

He looked at her incredulously, as though she'd taken leave of her mind. 'You weren't walking for seven hours. You'd have no shoe leather left.'

'Was it that long? I didn't notice the time. But of course I wasn't walking all night. I went to a cinema in town.'

'What film did you see?'

Her mind went blank. 'Oh, I don't recall the title,' she said airily. 'It was very boring, really. Nothing that you'd be interested in, I'm sure. Though there's no accounting for taste.' She had reached the top of the stairs now and she made her way towards her room, hesitating a little before she pushed open the door. He was still by her side; he wasn't letting her out of his sight. 'Goodnight, Daniel.'

She started to turn away from him but he reached for her, his hands closing on her arms. 'You're cold,' he said, and there was surprise in his voice and a tinge of anger, too.

'You were so anxious to get away that you didn't even think to take a coat or sweater with you. What the hell were you thinking of? You've never just walked out like that before. I've been worried out of my mind. I had no idea where you were or when you might be back. I thought you might have had an accident. Didn't you even care what I might be thinking?'

'I didn't think you'd notice I'd gone. I had no idea

how long you'd be closeted with Miss Franklin—she is a "Miss", isn't she? I didn't imagine she could be married...or not happily at any rate, judging by all the come-to-bed looks she was giving you.'

His eyes widened. 'You're jealous,' he said, and laughed suddenly.

'Of course I'm not jealous,' she denied stiffly, pulling away from him. 'What utter nonsense. Why on earth would I be jealous? I just thought that from the looks of things you'd be occupied for some time and wouldn't want to be disturbed. So I went. Without telling you.' She pushed open the door, averting her face so that he wouldn't see the betraying colour that flushed her cheekbones. 'And now I'm going to bed. Goodnight.'

She said it with a finality that should have put an end to discussion but when she tried to close the door behind her she found that he was still there; he had followed her into the room.

'You're jealous,' he said again, taking her into his arms and kicking the door shut behind him with the heel of his shoe.

Sarah tried to struggle but he wasn't letting her go anywhere and his gleaming eyes told her that she could deny her emotions till the cows came home but he wasn't going to believe her.

'Let go of me, Daniel,' she protested. 'It isn't at all the way it looks. I was just surprised, that's all. I've heard about these women in your life—one in every country you've visited, isn't there? But I've never seen one in action before and I'm just amazed at how easy it all seems. A few smouldering looks and you were panting at her heels, ready to slide off into a cosy little love-nest. If you think I'd want to follow that you must be out of your head.'

'You're cold,' he murmured, chafing her arms with his hands, and she wondered helplessly if he had listened to a word she'd said.

'Daniel—' She broke off as he urged her gently but firmly backwards towards the bed.

'Sit down,' he said, pushing her into the softness of the mattress and coming to sit alongside her. He wrapped her in the duvet and held her against him, his hands still stroking, sliding down her body so that there was no part of her that didn't receive the benefit of those warming caresses.

'Daniel—'

'You should know better than to believe what you read in the papers,' he said. 'Yes, I've travelled and, yes, I've known a few women but I'm definitely not a roving Casanova. I've known Marty for some time; we work together.'

Sarah opened her mouth to say something but he placed his finger over her lips and she mumbled against that instead. It was hard to imagine work being on Marty Franklin's mind for very long when she was around Daniel.

'We talked about work for a few minutes,' he said, 'then she had to leave to get on a train for London.'

Sarah muttered again, thinking that she'd like to bite that restricting finger. She had Miss Franklin's number well enough. She might not have had all the time she needed today but she'd put Daniel on hold.

'I came looking for you,' Daniel murmured. 'You

hadn't even cleared away your equipment and that wasn't at all like you. You're always so neat and efficient and you're usually so coolly in control of everything you do. Except when it comes to looking after donkeys, of course, but that was another kind of situation altogether.'

He removed his finger at last and she said tautly, 'You're laughing at me and I don't think this is at all funny. Will you let go of me? I'm perfectly warm now and I'd like you to leave. I'd like some privacy.'

'You put me through hell tonight,' he pointed out in a thickened voice. 'Why should I listen to you?'

'Because I—'

The trill of the phone cut across her words and, when Daniel would have ignored it, she said crossly, 'Answer it, for heaven's sake, or it might go on all night.'

The receiver was next to him on the bedside table and he obligingly lifted it.

'Courtenay here.'

She heard Philip's voice and blinked in surprise.

'I know it's late,' Philip said, 'but I need to talk to Sarah.'

'She's in bed,' Daniel said grittily, and Sarah glared at him.

'Give me the phone,' she demanded in a harsh whisper but he ignored her.

'Can't it wait till morning?' he said to Philip.

'No, I'm afraid it can't.'

He handed the receiver over to Sarah and she said hurriedly, 'Philip, is everything all right? It isn't like you to ring at this time of night.'

There was a pause and for a moment she thought he must have put the phone down. Then he asked curtly, 'Is he in the room with you? What the hell is he doing in there with you?'

Sarah sucked in a deep breath, aware of Daniel's arm still firmly wrapped around her, his blue gaze mocking. She tried to shift away from him but he wasn't letting her go anywhere.

'It isn't what you think, Philip, but I'll explain later. What is it you want? Are you ringing from Wellbrook?' She had forgotten that he was expected home from his trip any day now. She had hardly given him a thought these last couple of weeks and that made her feel hot with shame.

'Yes, I'm ringing from Wellbrook.'

Something in his tone made her stiffen. 'Has something happened? Tell me.' Even as she said it she thought of her father and her fingers tightened till the knuckles went white. 'My father—'

'Your father has been taken to hospital,' Philip said, his voice sounding remote. 'He had a heart attack about an hour ago.'

CHAPTER NINE

'I'LL drive you,' Daniel said, when Sarah had thrown her things into a case and was searching for her keys.

'I can manage.'

'No, you can't. You're anxious and overwrought and the last thing you need right now is to be driving yourself.' His jaw was set in an obstinate line and she knew that there would be no arguing with him. 'I'll arrange to have your car brought to you tomorrow,' he suggested, 'if that's what's bothering you.'

'What's bothering me is the fact that my father has had a heart attack and I wasn't with him,' she told him unhappily. 'It might never have happened if I'd been there to keep an eye on him. I should never have come here.'

'You weren't to know this would happen. You can't nursemaid him the whole time.' Daniel picked up her case and strode with it across the hall.

'I knew he'd been under a strain. I should have done more; I should have tried to make things easier for him.' Her mouth compressed into a bitter line. 'I should have kept you away from him.'

Daniel marched outside in silence. His car was parked in front of the Hall and he swiftly loaded up the boot and slammed the lid down.

Sarah stared back at the house. She'd had no idea

when she'd come here that she would be leaving in such circumstances as these. Overnight it seemed as though her world was crumbling around her.

'Get in the car,' Daniel ordered tersely. 'There won't be much traffic at this time of night so it shouldn't take us too long to get there.'

The hospital was quiet when they arrived. Reception was lit up but on the wards the night lights were glowing palely amber and the patients were sleeping, or at least trying to get some rest. Her father was in a coronary unit and the nurse in charge allowed Sarah and Daniel to go quietly into his room.

'Don't try to talk to him,' she warned. 'He's sleeping and that's what he needs right now.'

Margaret was already there, sitting by the bedside, and she hugged Sarah as she walked into the room.

'It seemed to come on so quickly,' she said in a hushed, tearful voice. 'He'd been all right earlier in the evening. At least, I didn't see much sign of anything wrong—except that he looked a bit tired. Then Philip came to see him around nine o'clock and I was glad because I thought having a man around the place to talk to would be good for him. I thought it might perk his spirits up a bit, with him being a bit low, just lately. Then, about eleven, this happened.'

Sarah felt a lump clogging her throat as she looked at her father. He was so pale and there were wires attached to him, leading to various monitors. She felt so helpless, seeing him lying there. She brushed the moisture from her eyes and sat with him, on the other side of the bed from Margaret, holding his hand gently in both of hers.

Nurses came and went and she had no idea how long she sat there. No one was saying very much in that room and it was only after the doctor visited and she began to stir from her lethargy that she realised she had hardly spoken a word to Daniel. She had been so bound up in her own unhappiness that she had simply accepted his calm, quiet presence.

It was selfish of her to take him for granted and now she turned to him and whispered, 'I want to stay here with him until I know he's out of danger. You don't need to keep me company. I expect you must want to get back.'

'I'm not going anywhere,' he said. 'If there's anything you and Margaret need, just ask and I'll get it for you. You both look white as sheets. How about a coffee? There's a machine in the corridor.'

'Thanks. I dare say we could all do with a drink.' For all that she had suggested he go, she did feel better knowing that he was staying. When she thought back to what she'd said earlier, remembering how she'd blamed him, she knew that somehow she had to make amends.

Margaret went out to use the washroom and when Daniel returned with the coffee, Sarah said softly, 'What I said to you earlier...about keeping you away from him...I shouldn't have blamed you, I know that, really. It wasn't your fault. No one could have prevented this.'

'You were very distressed,' he acknowledged

evenly. 'If there had been a way I could have helped your father, I would have found it. But you know, as well as I do, that he's a proud man. Stubborn, too. I could hardly have waived the whole debt. He was set on paying. As it was, I tried to make it as easy on him as I could. He was the one who insisted on getting wound up about it. My mother never harassed him and neither did I, though I know it looked that way to you.'

'I never understood why your mother would have lent him such an amount.'

'Neither did I until recently. But I think I ought to leave your father to explain that.'

'Do you think he looks a bit better?' she asked doubtfully. 'His colour seems to be improving, don't you think?'

'It does.'

As they spoke her father stirred, opening his eyes and slowly focusing on the two of them.

'How are you feeling?' Sarah asked quietly. 'Margaret will be so glad you're awake. She's just slipped off to the washroom.'

'I'm so sorry, Sarah,' her father said, his voice barely above a whisper. 'I've made such a mess of things. It was bad enough to make a hash of my own life but now I've messed up yours too.' His breathing was laboured and she tried to quieten him.

'Take things easy, Dad. Don't try to talk.'

'But it's all my fault. Can you patch things up with Philip, do you think? He was so angry and you can't blame him for that.'

Philip...angry? Sarah was confused. She'd wondered why he wasn't here at the hospital, though deep down she was glad he'd stayed away. The truth was that it was Daniel she needed to be with now. Somehow she thought she could get through anything with Daniel by her side.

Philip had sounded tense on the phone and that was understandable if he thought that she had been sharing a bed with another man. Strange behaviour for a woman who was to be engaged on her birthday. But she had said she would explain...and it was hardly likely that he'd passed on the news to her father. Besides, her father had already had his heart attack by then.

'How can it be your fault?' Sarah said, trying to smile. 'You mustn't lie here worrying. You have to concentrate on getting better.'

'It was the accounts,' William said. 'The shop's turnover was so low that no one was going to take on the shop. So I...' he swallowed painfully, trying to get the words out '...so I altered the accounts to make it look as though things were better than they really were. I knew I shouldn't have done it but I was desperate. I wasn't thinking straight.'

He stopped to draw in a rasping breath. 'There was the house to think of. It's Margaret's home. I owe it to her to keep it. That's why the loan was made—so I could buy the shop and make a reasonable income to keep a decent roof over her head after our parents died.

'We'd never had much money and a lot of Margaret's income had gone into paying off their debts. Daniel's mother always felt that Margaret should have been better provided for but I suppose she couldn't go openly against Daniel's grandmother. I've let her down—I've let everyone down. I've never made a go of the shop. It just drained money like sand through a sieve.' He swallowed hard.

'I thought that if I altered the accounts I'd get it off my hands and the new owners would make a better job of it than I had. Only Philip's parents found out what I'd done... I'm so sorry, Sarah. He was very angry and it's only natural that he should be.'

Sarah said shakily, 'You must rest and forget about everything that's happened. All I want is for you to get well again. I'll talk to Philip in the morning and we'll sort things out between us but you must try not to worry any more. Promise me you'll try to rest.'

'I'll try.' He sighed heavily. 'I am very tired.'

She gave his hand a gentle squeeze and he closed his eyes and after a while he slipped back into sleep. Sarah stared down at him, her mind in turmoil, until Daniel put an arm around her and drew her away from the bed.

'I think it's time you went home and tried to get some rest yourself. You'll think more clearly in the morning.'

'I agree,' Margaret said decisively, and they both turned, startled to realise that she had crept quietly into the room without either of them noticing. 'I had a word with the doctor and he thinks he's stabilised for now. He doesn't think there's any need for us to stay here any longer tonight. We'll come back tomorrow when we're all feeling fresher.'

'I'll take both of you home,' Daniel said.

They walked out of the hospital, all of them silent, occupied with their own thoughts.

As they approached the car park, Daniel asked, 'Did you come by taxi, Margaret, or did Philip drop you off here?'

'Philip brought me. I think, from what I heard William say, his conscience must have been troubling him.'

He sent her a sharp look. When they reached his car he held open the door for her and said, 'Exactly how much did you hear back there?'

'Enough,' she muttered, sliding into her seat and strapping herself in. 'Why didn't anyone tell me what was going on? Did William seriously think that I hadn't suspected something through all these years? Just looking at us, anyone could see that we bear not the slightest resemblance to each other. And I certainly look nothing like our parents.'

Sarah turned around in her seat to stare at her. Margaret was always so matter of fact, and she was saying things now that appeared to make very little sense. Unless—

'Sarah didn't know,' Daniel commented wryly, getting in behind the wheel and starting up the engine. 'And neither did I until a few weeks ago. I imagine everyone thought you'd be upset, finding out the truth after all these years.'

'Tosh,' Margaret said rudely. 'There's been far too much pussyfooting around. Your grandmother must have had an iron will to be able to lord it over so many people for so long. I knew something wasn't right. For years I suspected that I'd been adopted but no one would ever tell me the truth. Well, now I know. What does that make you, Daniel? My nephew?'

'Welcome to the fold, Aunt Margaret.'

Sarah's mouth twisted oddly. 'Your mother was the seamstress? You've never sewn a decent seam in your life!'

'We can't inherit all our parents' skills and talents, now, can we? I dare say there's a lot of my father in me. Daniel will have to tell me all about him when things quieten down a bit and we can get back to normal.' She caught his glance in the car's mirror. 'You'll stay at the cottage tonight, won't you?'

'That would make life easier. Thanks.'

Early next morning Sarah phoned the hospital. Her father's condition had improved slightly but he was to rest quietly through the morning and they would be allowed to visit him in the afternoon.

She relayed the news to Margaret, then checked her watch. 'I'm going over to Stoneleigh House to see Philip.' She added, conscious of Daniel's dark gaze resting on her, 'I'll be back in plenty of time to go with you to the hospital.'

'You're going to sort things out with him,' Margaret said flatly. 'He'll need to look at what your father did in a different light if you're to be married.' She left the table and went towards the kitchen door.

'I'll be in the garden. It's peaceful there, and I need some time to get myself together.'

The door closed behind her, and Daniel got to his feet. 'Are you sure that you want to see him alone? That might not be a wise thing to do. I could drive you.'

'I'll take Dad's car. And there's no need for you to come along; I'm not afraid of Philip. He loves me. If he was to see you with me it would probably make matters ten times worse—but you knew there would be trouble when you took the call from him last night, didn't you? You wanted him to think we were in bed together.'

'It would have been a fact sooner or later, no matter how much you try to deny it.'

She couldn't deny it but she turned away from him now so that he wouldn't see the faint trembling of her mouth and realise how far his words had struck home.

'I must go,' she said, reaching for her jacket. 'Philip's number's by the telephone just in case there should be a call from the hospital. Talk to Margaret, will you, when she comes in from the garden? For all that she pretends to be tough, I think she's had a big shock and you could probably help her get over it more than most. She needs to talk about her real family.'

'I'll do what I can. What are you going to say to Philip?'

'I don't know yet.'

It was going to be another warm day, with the sun's glow already appearing through a hazy early morning sky, but Sarah felt only a deep chill inside her as she drove to Stoneleigh House. She hadn't phoned Philip but it was the weekend and he wasn't likely to be at the factory.

'Could we go down to the Lodge to talk?' she asked him when he answered her knock at the door.

Philip nodded briefly, walking with her along the drive and letting them both into the house that was to be theirs.

'How is he?' he asked.

'Holding his own,' she said quietly. 'You didn't stay at the hospital. I wondered if I might see you there but Margaret said you dropped her off.'

'William was in good hands. There wasn't anything more I could do by staying around.'

'Not for him, perhaps, but Margaret and I might have welcomed some support. Didn't you think of that?'

Philip shrugged uncomfortably. 'I don't like hospitals. They smell of antiseptic and they make me feel depressed.'

'And it wouldn't do at all for you to be depressed, would it?'

A tinge of red crept into his cheeks. 'I don't know what call you have to talk to me like that, Sarah. I'm the one who's been ill used in this situation. I called you when William had his heart attack and what did I find? You were in bed and Courtenay was with you.'

'I told you it wasn't the way it seemed. Daniel was winding you up. I was in the bedroom, yes, though I wasn't in bed and Daniel was there, talking to me, but we were both fully dressed.'

He made a gruff sound, deep in his throat, a mixed reaction that she couldn't decipher.

'Perhaps that can be explained away, but what about this business of the bookshop? I tried to help you and your father by arranging for my parents to take an interest in it and look what I got for my trouble. Your father did something that was fraudulent and my parents are very angry.'

'I'm sorry,' Sarah said. 'He knows that he made a terrible mistake.'

'That's all very well, but it may not be just my parents who found out what he did. The agent said someone else had expressed an interest in the property and if he decides to go ahead with the purchase he could just as easily discover what William has done. If the sale goes ahead and he finds out later that the figures are wrong, he might be justified in taking the matter to court.'

It was what she had feared but she had hoped that Philip wouldn't have found it necessary to put it into words. She had hoped that the threat might somehow fade away.

'I hope it won't come to that. Perhaps you could talk to your parents—try to make them see how desperate he was and how sorry he is now for what he did?'

Philip looked at her peevishly. 'I don't understand you, Sarah. You must understand our position. We can't be seen to be involved with bad practices. If he's capable of doing it once he's likely to try something similar another time and sooner or later he will finish up by being prosecuted. Mud will fly around, and some of it will stick.

'As things are, you and I will have to postpone our engagement for some time—till this has all died down and you've managed to dissociate yourself from what your father has done. You'd come and live at the Lodge, of course; then after about a year we could maybe think about continuing with our plans.'

Sarah stared at him. 'You're serious, aren't you? You really mean me to sever connections with my father?' She shook her head wonderingly. 'Daniel was right all along. You *are* a cold fish. How could I ever have thought that you were the man for me— the man that I could want to spend the rest of my life with?'

'It seems to me,' Philip said huffily, 'that Courtenay has had much too great an influence on you since he came on the scene. You've changed, you know. But he'll go away, back to Houghton Wood, and you'll forget all about him in time and things will settle down to the way they were. You're not yourself, right now, Sarah. You've been under a strain and you don't know what you're saying. You have to be sensible and think of your future—of our future together.'

'You're right,' she said, 'and that's exactly what I'm doing. We don't have a future together, you and I. I must have been blind not to see that. There won't be an engagement, Philip. Not now; not ever. I'm sorry your parents had to find out what my father did and I'm sorry that you find it all so hard to stomach.

'Unfortunately I have to live with it. I love my father, no matter what he's done, and I've come to realise that it isn't love I feel for you at all. We've been friends and I shan't ever forget the happy times we shared together but it's time for a parting of the ways.' She walked swiftly to the door. 'Goodbye, Philip.'

She heard him call after her as she hurried down the drive but she kept on going until she reached the car and she didn't look back once. She drove away, going back to the cottage, and she was ashamed that all she felt in her heart was overriding relief.

Daniel was helping Margaret organise lunch in the kitchen when she returned. From the appetising smells that drifted on the air she could tell that he knew what he was doing but for the life of her she couldn't have eaten anything. She was far too wound up.

'There's a basket of fruit in the hall,' she said to nobody in particular. 'Is it a treat for Dad? It's huge. It'll take him a month to get through it.'

'It is,' Daniel said, looking at her keenly.

Sarah supposed that her eyes must be over-bright and her voice was a little off key. She felt unreal, as though everything around her had taken on a dream-like quality and she was teetering on a knife-edge of conflicting emotions. She was afraid that she was fast losing control.

'I have something for you,' Daniel said. 'I put it

upstairs in your bedroom where it would be cool. Come and see.'

She went with him. He had bought her a bouquet of red roses—each one a furled bud, each one perfect—with a fragrance that teased her nostrils even before she set foot in the room. She was overwhelmed that he should have made such a thoughtful gesture. He thrust the flowers into her hands and she said brokenly, 'They're so beautiful. . . so perfect. I don't deserve these. What have I done to deserve these?'

'Does there have to be a reason?' he asked with a smile. 'Though, if you're searching for one, I did ask Margaret some time ago when your birthday would be coming around. She has a present for you downstairs. Had you forgotten it was today?'

'Oh!' Her fingers went to her mouth in startled remembrance. 'So much has been happening these last few days. It went completely out of my head.'

But it didn't matter that it was her birthday. Daniel's gift was that he cared; he had taken the trouble to enrich her life with his thoughtfulness. She buried her face in the blooms, drinking in their sweet scent and feeling the slow tears begin to trickle down her cheeks.

She didn't know why she was crying but it didn't seem to matter. He took her in his arms, his hand splayed out on the silkiness of her hair, drawing her head down on to his chest so that the tears dampened his shirt and the flowers were crushed between them.

'Tell me what happened,' he said. 'Didn't Philip want to see reason? Is that why you're upset?'

She shook her head, rubbing her hot brow against his chest. 'It isn't that,' she managed between muffled sobs.

'What then?'

'The flowers are so lovely,' she said thickly, fresh tears falling. 'No one's ever bought me roses before.'

She felt his smile on her cheek. 'I'm not surprised if this is the way you're going to react.' He brushed the hair back from her temple and tilted her chin so that he could look down into her eyes.

She lifted a hand to wipe the dampness from her cheeks. 'We're spoiling them,' she said huskily. 'The poor things will be ruined before I get the chance to put them in water. Perhaps I'd better rescue them while you have lunch. We ought to be on our way to the hospital. I want to see for myself how Dad's doing.'

He released her with obvious reluctance and she went into the bathroom to splash water over her face and get herself back together again. When she went downstairs some minutes later Margaret and Daniel were ready to leave.

Her father looked much brighter than he had done the day before and over the next week it was satisfying to see how much of his strength he was regaining. He was far more cheerful and a lot of that had to be down to Daniel who was spending a lot of time talking to him, playing cards with him, or simply reading the newspaper and airing opinions.

Daniel was still staying over at the cottage and

Sarah was glad of that for Margaret's sake. The school holidays had begun, and she would no longer have work to take her mind off things. It was easier for Sarah in a way. She had to go to the shop every day and there was always something that she could find to occupy herself with when she was there.

Daniel would have liked to spend time with her, she knew, but she was avoiding being alone with him whenever possible. Her emotions were fluctuating wildly; sometimes she felt that without him life would be unbearable and at other times she knew that she had to distance herself because soon he would be gone from here and it wasn't likely that he would be looking back.

'You must be pleased that your father's coming home tomorrow,' he said as they were returning from a visit to the hospital.

'I am. He's looking a lot better but he'll improve by leaps and bounds once he's back on his own territory.'

Daniel drew the car to a halt and let Margaret out. Her friend was waiting at the gates of the park and they both turned and waved as the car moved off again.

'I'll be moving back to the Hall, then. When you get the chance you must come over.'

She had known that he would go sooner or later. She had just hoped that it wouldn't be sooner. 'I will,' she agreed. 'I haven't forgotten that I still have the work to finish for you.'

Daniel gave her a dry, sideways glance. 'I wasn't thinking about the work. I'd like you to visit and it would do you good to get out and about a bit. You can't go on pining for Philip for ever.'

'Pining?' Her brows drew together, a faint, crooked line working its way down her brow. 'What gave you the idea that I was doing that?'

'Aren't you? You were very upset after you spoke to him on your birthday and since you haven't seen him once to my knowledge since that day I assume things must be over between you. You've hardly left the cottage, except to go to the shop or the hospital. You should have been wearing his ring by now but you aren't and I don't believe it's because you're waiting for your father's health to improve.'

'You've been making a lot of assumptions, haven't you?'

'If you won't talk to me about it, then what else is left?' He parked the car outside the cottage and waited until they were in the house before he added, 'He would only have made you unhappy if you'd stayed with him. You might have seemed to share similar interests on the surface but deep down, where it counts, you were chalk and cheese.'

'I know. That's why I ended things between us.'

He gave her a narrowed, dark look as she walked into the sitting room. 'You're not regretting doing that?'

'No. I feel ashamed to say it but I'm relieved that it's over. You were right all along. We would never have suited. I don't know why it took me so long to see that.'

Sarah sat down on the plump-cushioned sofa,

suddenly weary. He was going back to the Hall, he'd said, and she couldn't think beyond that.

'I seem to have been waiting an age for you to say that,' Daniel murmured, coming to sit beside her. 'I wanted him out of the way, out of your mind. But you know that, don't you? You know how I feel about you?'

She said slowly, 'I know that you want me. I knew that almost from the first. It's why I was so wary of you. I'd heard you weren't the type to stay long in one place.'

'What kind of life could I have offered any woman? I was always on the move—that's the nature of my job. Women want at least the promise of security, permanency, but I was never able to give that. I never cared for anyone enough.'

'I know. I expect you'll stay on the move for years to come.'

'I don't think so.' His blue glance moved over her warmly, like a caress. 'I love you, Sarah. I've never needed anyone before but I need you. I want you, yes...by my side, for always, as my wife. Will you marry me?'

He touched her hand lightly, drawing it into his own, and she looked up at him with shimmering, stricken eyes. 'I can't,' she whispered unhappily. 'I can't.'

'Why can't you? Don't you love me?' Her lashes flickered downwards, hiding her expression, and he cupped her face with his hand, making her look at him. 'Why, Sarah?'

'It wouldn't be fair to you,' she got out in a

strained tone. 'You're in the public eye, and it wouldn't do for you to be connected with me. Philip warned me that news of what my father did might get out and word spreads fast round here. There would be a scandal. I can live with that but I can't expect you to share it. It could ruin you.'

Daniel swore softly. 'It's time you stopped letting Philip organise your life. A breath of scandal might bother him but it certainly doesn't bother me. The Courtenays are no strangers to scandal—Margaret is living proof of that. Besides, it isn't very likely that word of what your father did is going to be bandied about. The Prescott-Searles certainly don't want any adverse publicity.'

'But I don't know who else has seen the accounts. Someone else was interested in buying before all this blew up.'

'Someone else still is.'

She stared at him, open-mouthed. 'You?'

'That's right. I was thinking about buying the place when you came over to stay at the Hall. I needed to work out a way of keeping your father in the driving seat and at the same time show him how to turn the shop into making a profit.'

'And did you?'

He smiled crookedly. 'I spent a long time talking to your father while he was in hospital. We decided that we might expand what's on offer. Include antiques, paintings—broaden the canvas a bit. I'll be there as a sleeping partner, so to speak. Ready with advice, contacts, and so on. We think it should work well.'

Sarah lifted her hands to his face, brushing her thumbs lightly across his cheekbones. She needed desperately to touch him. 'You're a wonderful man,' she said softly. 'I could spend the rest of my life loving you.'

'Is that a promise?'

'It's a promise,' she breathed fervently.

'I think promises like that should be sealed with a kiss, don't you? Two kisses, maybe...three... four...' Daniel tilted her back against the cushions of the sofa and for long, blissful moments she lost herself in honeyed, rapturous sensation as their mouths met and clung.

His hands were moving over her, sweeping over every curve and line, engulfing her in flame. She needed to be closer; she wanted him so much that she was aching with need, the soft plea for more trembling on her lips.

Her own fingers tugged at his shirt. 'A kiss isn't nearly enough,' she whispered passionately, her mouth tracing a fiery path over his bared chest. Her tongue flickered hungrily across his smoothly muscled skin and he groaned thickly.

'Not nearly enough,' he echoed. Their clothes were lost somewhere in the breathless excitement of their passion for each other and he was kissing her now with growing intimacy, tasting the curving sweetness of her breasts, his lips brushing each aroused, sensitive nub in turn until she thought that she might faint with the ecstasy of it.

Her heart was racing out of control. She was poised on the edge of some fiery vortex and when he made her his, completely, utterly, she was consumed by flame. Desire exploded within her—a pleasure so intense that his name broke from her in tiny gasps, her fingers curling into the taut muscles of his shoulders.

He was with her in that chasm of fire, the searing lick of flame spiralling around them until, with the ragged, heated exhaustion of joyous fulfilment, they subsided together into delicious languor.

Sarah was the first to rouse herself, leaning up on one arm, the fingers of her free hand playfully roaming across his chest. 'I expect Margaret will be back soon,' she murmured. 'I wonder how she'll take the news of our getting married?'

'It won't come as any surprise to her,' Daniel answered in a huskily amused tone. He captured her straying fingers and drew them to his lips.

'It won't?'

'No way. She already told me we'd spent far too long shilly-shallying about and I was to get a move on. She said that she wanted at least four weeks' notice of any wedding so that she could get it organised properly. And since she expected it to be this summer she was looking at the wedding fabrics on offer in town and she'd have a good supply of samples for you to choose from.

'Not that she expects you to make your own dress, of course. She does know a very skilled woman who lives on the east side of Wellbrook. All you have to do is choose your design.'

Sarah chuckled softly. 'Isn't that just like Aunt

Margaret? I think a summer wedding would be so romantic, don't you?'

'That's exactly what I told her,' Daniel agreed, wrapping his arms securely about her and placing a tender kiss on her soft mouth.

MILLS & BOON®

Something new and exciting is happening to...

Medical Romance™

From August 1996, the covers will change to a stylish new white design which will certainly catch your eye!

They're the same Medical Romance™ stories we know you enjoy, we've just improved their look.

PRESCRIPTION - ONE HUSBAND
MARION LENNOX

---

4 titles published every month at £2.10 each

*Available from WH Smith, John Menzies, Volume One,
Forbuoys, Martins, Woolworths, Tesco, Asda, Safeway
and other paperback stockists.*

MILLS & BOON®

Back by Popular Demand

BETTY NEELS

COLLECTOR'S EDITION

A collector's edition of favourite titles from one of the world's best-loved romance authors.

Mills & Boon are proud to bring back these sought after titles, now reissued in beautifully matching volumes and presented as one cherished collection.

Don't miss these unforgettable titles, coming next month:

Title #7   THE MOON FOR LAVINIA
Title #8   PINEAPPLE GIRL

Available wherever
Mills & Boon books are sold

Available from WH Smith, John Menzies, Forbuoys, Martins, Tesco, Asda, Safeway and other paperback stockists.

MILLS & BOON®

From Here To Paternity

Don't miss our great new series featuring fantastic men who eventually make fabulous fathers.

Some seek paternity, some have it thrust upon them—all will make it—whether they like it or not!

In August '96, look out for:

Grounds for Marriage
by Daphne Clair

Available from WH Smith, John Menzies, Volume One, Forbuoys, Martins, Woolworths, Tesco, Asda, Safeway and other paperback stockists.

GET 4 BOOKS AND A MYSTERY GIFT

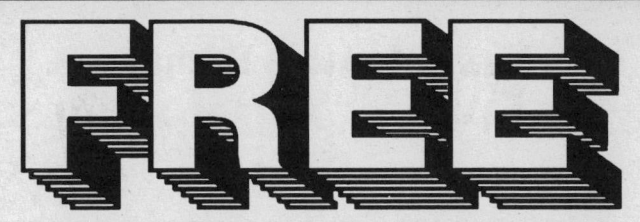

FREE

Return this coupon and we'll send you 4 Mills & Boon® romance novels and a mystery gift absolutely FREE! We'll even pay the postage and packing for you.

We're making you this offer to introduce you to the benefits of Reader Service: FREE home delivery of brand-new Mills & Boon romance novels, at least a month before they are available in the shops, FREE gifts and a monthly Newsletter packed with information.

Accepting these FREE books and gift places you under no obligation to buy, you may cancel at any time, even after receiving just your free shipment. Simply complete the coupon below and send it to:

MILLS & BOON READER SERVICE, FREEPOST, CROYDON, SURREY, CR9 3WZ.

No stamp needed

Yes, please send me 4 free Mills & Boon Romance novels and a mystery gift. I understand that unless you hear from me, I will receive 6 superb new titles every month for just £2.10* each postage and packing free. I am under no obligation to purchase any books and I may cancel or suspend my subscription at any time, but the free books and gifts will be mine to keep in any case. (I am over 18 years of age)

2EP6R

Ms/Mrs/Miss/Mr _____

Address _____

_____

_____ Postcode _____

Offer closes 31st January 1997. We reserve the right to refuse an application. *Prices and terms subject to change without notice. Offer only valid in UK and Ireland and is not available to current subscribers to this series. **Readers in Ireland please write to: P.O. Box 4546, Dublin 24.** Overseas readers please write for details.

You may be mailed with offers from other reputable companies as a result of this application. Please tick box if you would prefer not to receive such offers. ☐

MILLS & BOON®

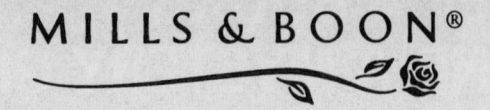

Next Month's Romances

Each month you can choose from a wide variety of romance with Mills & Boon®. Below are the new titles to look out for next month.

THE TROPHY HUSBAND	Lynne Graham
RENDEZVOUS WITH REVENGE	Miranda Lee
RUNNING WILD	Alison Fraser
MARRIAGE BY ARRANGEMENT	Sally Wentworth
A PROPER WIFE	Sandra Marton
INTIMATE RELATIONS	Elizabeth Oldfield
MOVING IN WITH ADAM	Jeanne Allan
GROUNDS FOR MARRIAGE	Daphne Clair
AMBER'S WEDDING	Sara Wood
HAVING IT ALL!	Emma Richmond
THE PERFECT MALE	Rosemary Hammond
FOR BABY'S SAKE	Val Daniels
ENTICED	Jennifer Taylor
VIRGIN TERRITORY	Suzanne Carey
AT FIRST SIGHT	Eva Rutland
COUNTERFEIT COWGIRL	Heather Allison

Available from WH Smith, John Menzies, Volume One, Forbuoys, Martins, Woolworths, Tesco, Asda, Safeway and other paperback stockists.